CEN

SACRAMENTO PUBLIC LIBRARY

3 3029 03207 5335

CENTRAL LIBRARY

JAN 3 0 1994

H. E. BATES
The Feast of July

H. E. Bates was born in 1905 in Northamptonshire, England. He worked as a journalist and clerk on a local newspaper before publishing his first novel, *The Two Sisters*, at the age of twenty. He established a reputation for his stories about English country life, and, later, for novels based on his wartime experiences in Burma and India. Author of the bestselling *Fair Stood the Wind for France* and *The Darling Buds of May*, he also wrote essays, short stories, plays, and an autobiography, and his works have been translated into sixteen languages. H. E. Bates was awarded the C.B.E. in 1973 and died in January 1974.

VINTAGE

INTERNATIONAL

Central Library
828 I Street
Sacramento, CA 95814-2589

ALSO BY H. E. BATES

The Two Sisters

Spella Ho

Fair Stood the Wind for France

The Cruise of the Breadwinner

The Purple Plain

The Jacaranda Tree

Dear Life

The Scarlet Sword

Colonel Julian and Other Stories

Love for Lydia

The Nature of Love

The Darling Buds of May

Central Library
828 I Street
Sacramento, CA 95814-2589

The Feast of July

The Feast of July

H. E. BATES

VINTAGE INTERNATIONAL

Vintage Books

A Division of Random House, Inc.

New York

FIRST VINTAGE INTERNATIONAL EDITION, SEPTEMBER 1995

Copyright © 1954 by H. E. Bates
Copyright renewed 1982 by Richard Bates and Jonathan Bates

All rights reserved under International and Pan-American
Copyright Conventions. Published in the United States by Vintage Books,
a division of Random House, Inc., New York. Originally published in
hardcover by Little, Brown and Company in association with
the Atlantic Monthly Press, Boston, in 1954.

Library of Congress Cataloging-in-Publication Data
Bates, H. E. (Herbert Ernest), 1905–1974.
The Feast of July / H. E. Bates. — 1st Vintage International ed.
p. cm.
ISBN 0-679-76501-8
I. Title.
PR6003.A965F43 1995
823'.912—DC20 95-8914
CIP

Manufactured in the United States of America
10 9 8 7 6 5 4 3 2 1

The Feast of July

I

SHE was looking for a man named Arch Wilson and she
was walking southwestward, alone, towards the middle
of the country, with another fifty or sixty miles to go.

All day, after two days and nights of rain, water had
been rising in the dykes and now it was creeping rapidly
up the five stone arches of the bridge where she stood
watching the wide rainy valley up which the tongue of
river finally lost itself in a gray country of winter elms.

Down below her was a boat, partly covered by a green
tarpaulin. She had some crazy idea that she could sleep
in the boat. As far as she could tell there were no oars in
it. The mooring chain was padlocked to an ash stake
driven in the mud. It was fifteen or twenty feet from the
boat to the water's edge and beyond it, high up, was an
open wooden shed. Inside the shed was a second boat
and she was wondering if the oars too could be there.
She was wondering too how hard a kick it would need to
break the ash stake out of the mud. Fifty or sixty yards
beyond the shed was a house, a low yellow-brick blue-
slated house with a big cheese of a grindstone standing in
the yard outside, and she was watching that too.

She walked along the bridge, slowly. She was not a tall girl but she walked as a tall girl does, upright, feeling her way, bare head thrown up and backwards. Her hands were small and slender. She was carrying everything she had in a black oilcloth bag she had taken from the cellar of the Three Bells Hotel, where she had been working all summer as a bedroom maid, and there was a smell of beer on the bag that the rain had still not washed away.

At the end of the bridge she stood for nearly five minutes watching for a sign from the house. All the time she was thinking that if only she could kick the stake out of the mud the boat would be easy. She could take it upstream for a mile or two and sleep under the tarpaulin. She was used to boats. From the windows of the Three Bells you looked across flat lands, downstream to the sea, and there were sea fish in the estuary. Men came down from towns in the upper valley for a week or two of fishing in the summer, hiring boats from the hotel, and Arch Wilson had been one of them in July.

"Arch Wilson. I'll be coming down again in a month. I'll drop you a card when I know the day."

In summer the wide flat lands were blue-gray with sea thistle. She remembered how the dry spines had pricked the bare gap of her thighs above her black stockings as she lay with him there under a breezy sky.

"You know what color your eyes are?"

"Green." She remembered laughing easily, as she always laughed in those days, with her tongue out. "That's every bit green you can see there."

[4]

"They're black," he said. "Black as cherries. That's what they are."

"They're green," she said, "all green when you talk to me."

"I'll be back in a month and I'll bring you a pair of shoes. Low shoes. *Glacé.*"

"I bet you'll never be back."

"August," he said. "The second week in August. What size are your feet?"

"You're a shoemaker. You ought to know."

"God, your eyes are black," he said and she laughed, again in the warm, easy, friendly way she had in those days.

But it was really the feeling of his hands on her stockinged feet, she remembered, and then the feeling of soft fresh sea wind on the bare skin of her legs that really woke her. She remembered beginning to tremble all over. "Threes," he said. "Narrow fitting. No bigger than a doll's."

She took a last look at the house and slid down the bank. At the foot of the bank she could see the print of earwig bores on the ash stake that held the boat and she knew that it was rotten. She kicked hard and felt her body wrench sharply as she turned and slipped in the mud but the stake split with a crack that woke a screaming voice from the yard behind the grindstone:

"You git outa there, burn you! I bin watching you! Git out on it!"

Along the bank a big gray woman came swinging a

hatchet in one hand and a split white billet of ash in the other.

"You git shut where you belong! You don't belong here, do you? You ain't from here, I know."

The girl was back up the bank, slithering in mud, running. The woman was running too, with big clubbing strides that shook her skirt, and the white cleft billet came flashing through the rainy air.

"We had boats nicked afore! Git out on it afore you git the chopper at you!"

The woman stood at one end of the bridge, coughing, breathing sharply through her teeth, long heavy arms swinging like a bear's. The girl stood at the other, turning, walking backwards.

"You're a rare-looking jinny an' all, ain't you? Where you from? Where's your hat?"

She came a yard or two farther up the crest of the bridge, menacing, coughing, swinging the hatchet.

"Where's your hat? That ain't it, is 't, under your ap'on?"

The girl turned her back, walking in her tall, upright fashion, feeling her way, black head held up.

"Ain't no use turning your back on me either. I can see. It's big enough."

She stood with the hatchet at her side, spitting.

"And you needn't gline back at me neither. You git no pity from me. You go an' lay where you should do afore you drop it in a field."

Through spits of rain the voice followed the girl for a

long time down the road. She stood for some time against a field gate, panting for breath, holding her body sickly, not caring about the rain. She felt the flooded fields swing about her in the darkening afternoon, blotting out her sense of direction, so that when she began to walk again it was the wrong way, stupidly and blindly, back toward the bridge.

It was only when she reached the bridge that she came to her senses. She was sharply aware then of another sound cutting harshly through the dying February afternoon.

It was the sound of the hatchet, shrill on the grindstone.

I I

SNOW began to fall a day later as she came to a higher
stretch of pasture country where the fields were no longer
divided by water dykes but by walls of stone. There were
many sheep in the fields in that part of the country and
as the wind sharpened, turning northwestward, spitting
at first little frozen bullets of snow, she saw them hud-
dling closer and closer under the lee of the walls, stone
and wool the same gray-yellow color against the pure
fresh snow.

By four o'clock in the afternoon the front of her body
was like a long curved white apron. Her skirt was of thick
heavy black serge that came down to her ankles and her
jacket was wide-shouldered, with big sleeves and frogs of
braid, black too, across the bodice. The only thing she
was wearing about her neck was a pair of black woolen
stockings she had taken out of her bag that morning and
underneath them a flat jet necklace. She was wearing the
necklace because it was something Arch Wilson had given
her and because she knew that he liked it.

"You said I wouldn't come back but I did. You said I
wouldn't bring the shoes but I did, didn't I?"

She had brought the small shining *glacé* shoes with her too in the sack. He had made them himself, he said. They had on them small square buckles of silvery metal, with insets of glittering glass that she thought were very beautiful, and in them her feet looked smaller and more delicate than ever.

"And I bought you something else," he said.

"What else? I don't want nothing else. The shoes are enough. The shoes are wonderful."

"I'll give it to you tonight," he said.

Her small slant-sided bedroom was in the top of the hotel; she had told him where it was. That night she could not sleep because she was so excited about the shoes and she remembered how she sat on the edge of the bed and looked at them over and over in the candlelight and how it seemed to her hardly possible to believe that there were such shoes.

Then he was in her room. "I came to ask you something," he said.

"You shouldn't come up here. People will hear. The landlord will hear. What is it you want to ask me?"

"I'm coming up again in a fortnight," he said. "What say we get married then?"

"Me? Married? You know how old I am? I'm eighteen. I'm only eighteen."

"You look older. You look like a woman already," he said.

Some time later she felt something against the cool skin of her throat in the darkness. "Guess what it is," he said. In the warm summer air the band of jet was cool on her throat and she began trembling again as he fastened it with his hands. It did not seem to her possible that a girl could be given such things as shoes and a necklace in a single day.

"I want to look at you," he said and presently she was lying there in the candlelight, with nothing on except the band of jet round her throat, her taut rounded young body stiffening and trembling and relaxing as he kept repeating her name:

"Bella. Bella. Oh! Bella," he said.

Under snow the afternoon began to darken early and some time after four o'clock she was sitting in a stone hovel that had a half-door and a roof thatched with black-thorn. There were many sheep clustered under the wall outside and under the lee of a haystack that stood beside a pond. Inside there was a bale or two of dry straw and a pile of swedes and in one wall a stone hearth with a chimney hole where fires had been made.

She had taken matches and candle from her bedroom and presently she was burning the broken slats of a sheep-hurdle, starting the fire with straw. She was afraid to light the candle but as she began to dry her bag and the things she had in it and then her high lace-up boots she felt more confident and no longer afraid. In her bag she had, besides her shoes and a picture of herself, a towel and half a loaf of bread and a knife and part of a bottle of small beer she had drawn from the cask in the cellar at the hotel.

She cut herself a slice of bread and then found a swede and cut a slice from the center of it and ate it with the bread. She could not hear the snow. Outside there was a queer wiry sound that she could not understand for some time until at last she knew it for the sound of wind scraping together the tall canes of reed that skirted the pond. When she stood by the half-door she could hear too the laboring breath of sheep as they grunted by the wall.

She did not know how late it was when she lay down in front of the fire on a pile of straw. She was not sleepy so much as stupefied and dazed and she could feel sometimes a pull of pain in her side, like a tightening knot, where she had slipped in the mud by the river.

She lay thinking again of Arch Wilson. "Everybody in Nenweald's a shoemaker," he said. "Or a tanner. They get the water from the river."

"Our river? The same one? This one?"

Yes, he told her, the same river, and it was afterwards when she remembered it that she knew the way she had to go. "I only have to follow the river," she thought, "I shall get to it in time if I follow the river."

As she remembered this she remembered her mother. "You git no pity from me. I ain't the pityin' sort. I got no pity." Her mother was a prematurely gray round-shoul-dered woman who had married a second time. Her step-father was an out-of-work carter who had sat for the whole winter with his feet on the steel kitchen fender, smoking a short blackened clay and spitting at the fire while her mother went out and worked at scrubbing. When spring

came her sister had left home to get married to a railway
clerk and a week later she herself had left to work in the
hotel. It was a very good job at the hotel; she was very
pleased to get it: sixteen pounds a year and three meals a
day and beer if she was a mind to have it every morning
at eleven o'clock with her bread and cheese.

Her sister was a placid, gentle, totally unaggressive
woman nearly ten years older than herself who cried a
great deal when she heard of the baby.

"You can have it here. You can live with us," she said.

"No: I'll find him. If he doesn't come to me I'll go to
him. I'll find him somehow."

"Yes, but how? — if he don't come? — where?"

"I'll find him."

"And what about money? You got nothing. You only
just started."

"I'll find him," she said, "if I have to walk it every step
of the way."

All the money she had in the end was a little over three
pounds, two of which her sister had given her and the
rest of which she had saved herself. It was hardly enough
for her food and lodging and train fare if she wanted to
come back again. That was why she had taken the train
for five miles and then had got out and started to walk,
glad that the morning was fine and bright and feeling
that if the weather and her luck held she could do the
journey in five or six days.

Then the rain came, driven down the valley on a cold
white-wind gale that hit the river into waves. It scoured

the flesh of her face as she walked against it. It blew away her hat on the second day and drowned it like a tossed black-sailed boat in a dyke high in flood. It tired her greatly and she faced it as obstinately as she had faced her sister, pleading first with Bella not to go and then, if she had to go, always to remember that she could come back to her.

"I'll be here. There'll be a bed for you here. If you don't find him you can always come back here."

"I'll find him," she said. "I'll find him if I have to walk the length of the country."

There was still another thing she remembered as she lay before the fire. It was the soft, thick, malty way he had of talking. She could still feel the slimy way the syllables folded themselves about her mind and her heart. The lips under the edges of the sharp brown mustache were full and fleshy and yet they hardly moved as they framed his words. The lids of his white-blue brilliant eyes also gave a slurred and casual effect to his way of looking at her. The unflickering too-brilliant pupils seemed always to lock her own eyes in a mesmeric glaze. "When you look at me like that," she had said, "I feel I can't get away. I don't want to. I feel you've always got me."

It was three or four hours later when she got up for the third time to break another of the hurdle slats to make up the fire. She tried to break the slat by scotching it against the wall and hitting it with her foot. This time the slat was springy and she slipped as she kicked it and a fresh pain stabbed up through her body as if the slat had impaled her.

She lay down by the fire again, half on her face, struggling with the pain, sweating. She felt the pain recede and advance in a series of dragging and regular waves. It was no longer like the gentle pull of the baby turning inside her: the sensation she had known all winter, discomforting and scaring her as she lay alone at night, really more a pain of the mind. It was now as if part of her body were being dragged away from her and after a time she turned on her back and lay with her feet against the wall, pressing them hard against the stone, moaning in sweat.

Then the fire began to go down and in the half-darkness she crawled about the floor searching for wood to make it up again. A thin drift of snow had blown in under the crack of the door again and she could hear the low wiry whistle of wind in the pond reeds. The swede she had cut open to eat with her bread lay on the floor, the cut side almost frozen, and as she touched it accidentally it woke a great shudder in her throat and the shudder in turn became the beginning of a great cold wave of fright because she did not know what to do.

"Oh! God. God, oh! God," she kept saying. Almost without knowing it she kept the swede in her hand, clutching it for the sake of something to hold, and once she bit her teeth into it so that she should not cry.

Then at last she began to cry. She remembered somehow taking off her thick serge skirt and half covering her face with it and screaming into it, weeping and terrified. She could feel the ooze of blood on her legs and the scorching of her calves through her stockings as she rolled against the fire. The pain of burning was almost a comfort against the pain of her body contracting and convulsing, and then presently she could feel even that no longer.

When she came to herself again the fire was out and the thin drift of snow under the doorway had grown to the shape of a scythe three or four inches high. Her face was covered with her skirt. She was still clutching the swede in her hands. Her feet were still pressed against the side of the stone fireplace and in the air, freezing and windless after snow, there was a sick dry odor of scorching where her stockings had burned.

After she had remembered the knife in the sack she lay there for a long time in the growing daylight, too weak to let it drop from her hands. She stared up at the black canopy of bushes that thatched the hovel and cried again without a sound or even a sensation of grief as she thought of Arch Wilson.

"If you were here I'd kill you," she thought. She felt the frozen draft of air cutting across the earth floor into her bloodless face. She felt herself sobbing in a stark space of emptiness, still clutching the knife in her hand.

"You did this to me," she thought. "You did this to me and if you were here I'd kill you."

She thought of the shoes and the necklace. She remembered the slurred malty voice talking to her as she lay among the sea thistle, in the summer, by the mouth of the river, under the waking sea wind. She remembered crying to him in the darkness "I'm eighteen, I'm only eighteen" and the way she had lain in the candlelight with nothing on her body but the jet necklace cool and black round her throat and the way he had called her name.

Outside she could hear, by this time, the sheep stirring and panting in the snow and she was suddenly ashamed and frightened that someone would arrive and find her there.

"I'll find you," she said. She lay in a pool of weakness where her bitterness was separate, outside of her, darkly and terribly apart. She was so tired that when she struggled first to her knees and then her feet, trying to put on her skirt, she could not hold the skirt and it dropped out of her hands as if they were paper.

"I was proud until this happened," she thought. "I had some pride until you did this to me."

Her sobbing, labored and choking, was like the echo of the waking sheep as they coughed dryly and harshly outside, in the snow.

"I'll find you. I'll find you and some day I'll kill you," she said.

It was more than a week later when she came up the long slope of the valleyside, between five and six in the evening, towards the outskirts of Nenweald. She still gave the impression of being taller than she was, walking with her head back, feeling her way. The snow of the week before had melted in most of the open places but under the high hedgerows it still lay in long pure slices and sometimes out in the open plowed clay lands it still stretched away in thin white bars.

She had got into a way of walking without thought, mindlessly, not troubling about distances. Her face had been fined down by exhaustion to pure bone with a taut covering of skin that was yellow and transparent, like a worn cake of soap. Her eyes were like a pair of smoky glasses and an unconscious habit of suddenly stabbing forward with her long thin hands, into empty air, made it seem as if she were frightened of falling down.

Walking like this she was surprised suddenly to see the town before her on the crest above the river. It was still not quite dark and in her pride she stopped by a gate to comb her hair. She had nothing to tie the straight mass of it back except a piece of her bootlace that had broken off two days before and her hands were still so weak that it was a long time before she could tie the knot securely.

Twice she let the lace fall through sheer weakness out of her hands. The second time, as she stooped to pick it up, groping in mud and snow, she felt the blood drain out of her face, leaving her faint and cold. She shut her eyes for a few moments, clinging to the gate, and when she opened them again she could see the first light on the edge of the town like a star.

Then as she stood knotting the bootlace she saw a curious thing. The star had repeated itself. Presently it was repeated four or five times, at regular intervals, in a line. She stood fascinated by the way this line became a curve, with a new dot of light sparking from it every thirty seconds or so, and it struck her that it was something like a little train uncurling its lighted carriages out of the bend of the valley.

Then she saw that the lights were turning, that the line was bending and coming towards her. She had begun to walk on by this time, passing the first houses and smelling in the damp twilight air the smell she was afterwards to know so well: the acrid greasy-sharp smoke of leather burning on evening fires. The causeway on the street-side was three or four feet up from the road and presently she was able to see that it was really a long line of street lamps, high on the causeway, that was marching towards her.

After some time a man of six feet or so, craggy at the knees and rather scurrying in the way he drew one thin tight-trousered leg quickly after the other, came out from under the line of lamps, carrying a long lamplighter's pole.

He went past her quickly, head up, breath hissing on the evening air, eyes not seeming to look at her. She heard the click of the gas chain in the nearest lamp below her; then the plop as the flame burst in the mantle. She turned to see the green fire of gaslight flooding the street and under it the lamplighter halting for a second or two, looking after her queerly, with a white glint of suspicion, mouth open.

She turned twice more, the second time just soon

enough to see him lighting the last of the lamps: a final green flower bursting against all the bare bright frostiness, a fierce wintry blue, above the valley. Then she heard him coming back: the quick scurried foot, the breath hissing as it sucked against the cold.

"Hanging about waiting for more to come," he said.

He was level with her now, in lamplight, squinting down over a long curved nose that bristled in the nostrils with abundant coils of furious yellow hairs.

She had not the slightest idea of what his sentence meant. She saw him look quickly down from her face to her boots. His breath hissed again, this time with excessive suddenness, as if he were pained or surprised or shocked by what he saw.

"You've been through some sludder," he said.

Sludder: a new word, a word she had never heard before. There was not the sign of a smile on his face as he spoke of the mud on her boots or, for the second time, of the snow.

"Much snow where you come from?"

"It was thick last week."

"Come far?" he said. "Addington way? Somewhere that way?"

"No," she said. "Farther back than that."

Her boots, her bag, the plaster of mud and snow on her long skirt, then the bootlace tying back her hair: she knew that, as she came to each of the lamps, he was looking at them all.

"You got kin here?"

"No," she said. "I got no kin here."

He seemed to ponder on that, not speaking again for some time. Off the street, at intervals, went stone passages that opened into yards, and at one of these he stopped.

"Wait for me," he said. "Don't go on. I got a lamp to do here."

She watched as he dragged his foot down the half-dark passage and she actually saw a spark from the heel of his boot as he turned under the lamp bracket at the far end. Then the same green flowering of light flooded down and he marched shadowily out of it, looking taller, gaunter than ever.

"That's Chapel Yard," he said. "That's our chapel."

He said something about lighting all the lights of the main street first and then the other lights, the lights in the yards, as he came back again. "We only had gas a year ago." He seemed very proud of the gas. He spoke as if all the lights belonged to him.

"Come visiting here?"

"No."

"Going on to Evensford then?" he said. "Gittin' as far as that?"

"No," she said. "This is where I'm stopping."

He paused again to light a lamp in a yard. She saw a low iron water tap, straw-covered against frost, dribbling under the light. He seemed annoyed by that. There was something righteous in the way he snarled down his nose about it and in the way his hand came out, long, black-nailed and hairy with masses of the same sandy-yellow coils as his nostrils.

"Folks urge you to death." His hand gave a broad sharp-tempered wrench to the tap, turning it off. She saw the last dribble of water cling to the lip of the tap, trembling there under gaslights, and it was almost like the last of her strength, quivering by a thread before it broke and dropped away.

Then she was in another yard, waiting for another break of light. Children, four little girls with flying pigtails and a boy with a flying brown scarf, were swinging by a rope at the lamppost, crying *Sally Go Round the Moon*. Light flooded down on them, making the hair of the little girls like yellow wings.

"Mr. Wainwright! Mr. Wainwright!" they called and he said:

"One time they didn't used to call me that. Lamplighter, flea-biter, that's what they used to say. Now they're better. They like me now."

She was hardly listening. The flying yellow pigtails rocketed round and round the lamppost like stiff bright-beating wings. Her head began to go round with them too, in strange, cold, sickening whirls, and she groped with her hand and clung blindly to the wall and heard him say:

"Ain't you well or something? You don't look very grand. Ain't you got nobody to go to?"

"Yes," she said. "I'm looking for a man named Arch Wilson."

"Wilson?"

He paused for some time before and after the word. Then he repeated it, slowly, and as she listened she felt herself drifting down the wall.

"Wilson? What Wilson would that be?"

"Arch Wilson. This is where he lives. He's a shoemaker."

"Shoemekker?" He had his own way of pronouncing that: sharpish, the voice rising, doubtful.

"This is where he lives. This is Nenweald — I know that. That's what they said."

"Nenweald," he said. "Yes: this is it. This is Nenweald. Arch Wilson? There used to be a man named Pug Wilson, but he worked at Jolly's mill. He was only a boychap. He went a-soldiering somewhere. Is this Arch Wilson a soldier?"

"I don't think so. I wouldn't think he was ever a soldier."

"Arch Wilson," he said.

He began to walk on, distracted by thought into forgetting for a moment that she was there by the wall. She felt herself desperately clinging to the stones behind her. She actually dug her nails into the joints of mortar as she forced herself upright so that she could follow him.

"Wait a minute," she said. "Wait. I'll tell you what he's like. He's a big man. Fresh-faced. A big fair man, about twenty-four."

"There ain't no Wilsons here," he said. "There ain't a Wilson in the town."

"No?"

He paused to light another bracket lamp on a street corner. The street was narrow, shabby, darkened by the walls of a factory, and she could smell the near odor of leather from beyond factory windows, not burning now but new and greasy and animal, sickening her.

As she stood there, sick, clinging to the bricks of the factory wall exactly as she had held on to the stones in the yards, she saw the big front doors of the factory open and a man in a white apron and a small black hard hat came out of it, carrying on his arm a big sleeve of boot uppers. The lamplighter called after him:

"Josh. Don't know no Wilson here, Josh, do you? Ain't ever heerd talk of Arch Wilson?"

"Wilson?" The man with the boot uppers wiped his free hand across the apron, dark-stained with finisher's black. "Ain't a Wilson in the town as I know on. Not 'ithout he's one of that new lot up at Spitalfields. There's a new lot just come up there."

As he went away into the darkness the flap of his white apron torn in a gust of wind brought home to her suddenly the clawing, frightening thought that she was alone in a strange town: that there was no Arch Wilson, that all she had done and been through, the rain, the boat, the woman with the chopper, the dead baby and the swede that was terribly like the face of the dead baby, were simply grotesque and terrible shadows of things that had never happened.

[23]

Then he said: "I got to get back home now. My name's Wainwright."

The thought that he was going to turn and vanish and leave her there rushed up into her throat, acidly, so that she began crying.

Then for the first time he touched her. She felt herself shudder. It was as if he had laid an enormous rod across her back.

"You better come home with me," he said. "We're a houseful as it is, but you can come." She saw the first commiserate touch of a smile, almost tender, on the ivory horselike teeth. "Come along o' me. We will see what we can do for you."

It seemed like a whole night, though it was less than half an hour, before she was sitting at a table, in a small back kitchen, in the light of a squat opaque oil lamp burned low, listening to Wainwright offering a prayer.

His voice, dried out, high-pitched, had a strained, wooden, uplifted sound. It was as unreal as the five other faces she saw with him there: the faces of three men, a woman and a girl crushed close together over the little oblong table as if the walls of the tiny room were pushing them inward in a common crouch of prayer.

"Bless this our sister." As Wainwright prayed she sat with open eyes, too exhausted to shut them, unaware that he was speaking of her. "Succor her if she is in trouble. Look down on her distress." A bright farthing of an enormous collar stud, jerkily impelled by a craggy Adam's apple, jumped up and down his throat. The prayer, groping and extempore, flared and jerked over and over again to what seemed its close, and then began again. "Forgive us if in our own ease, our own comfort, our own blindness, we have sometimes forgot — "

An eye woke across the table, watching her. It was no more than a narrow blue-and-white buttonhole and it closed again as she looked at it. In the center of the table, under the lamp, swam globes of pickled onions, like giant frog spawn packed in a glass, and they too seemed to be watching her. Wainwright prayed suddenly on a deep torn chord, almost a retch, of bursting fervor, entreating forgiveness in self-seeking: "We entreat thee. Oh! Lord we entreat thee — " and then she was aware of a spoon clipping the sides of a stewpot and the steam of onion broth in the air and she knew vaguely that the prayer was over.

When she could focus the table clearly again she saw five faces torn between the business of breaking bread into plates of broth and the curious task of watching her. Only Wainwright, half hidden behind the lamp, was not concerned with food.

"You didn't tell us your name," he said. He bent to the side of the lamp so that he could look at her.

"Isabella," she said. "My other name is Ford. Bella Ford."

"What did she say, Mother?"

"Bella, she says her name is. Bella Ford."

"Oh! Ford. Did you ever hear of a man named Arch Wilson, Mother?" he said. "Anywhere?"

"Not as I recollect."

Mrs. Wainwright, tiny, sparrow-sharp, with cheeks like polished eggshell, had a pale, severe, stoical brightness.

"That's Nell you're sitting next to," Wainwright said. "She would be about your age. How old would you be?"

"Twenty in the summer."

"Nell'll be nineteen next July. The week after Feast Sunday," Mrs. Wainwright said.

"And that's Jedd there." The son was heavy-boned and tall, like Wainwright himself, but more muscular, with a thick chest and the same water-blue eyes. His fair mustache was wax-pointed. His forehead was high and good-natured and had a quiff on it and Wainwright said: "He's our soldier. The cavalry. Home on furlough. You don't recollect any Arch Wilson here, do you, Jedd?"

"No, sergeant."

"That's what he calls me: sergeant," Wainwright said. He smiled the wide, uneven horse-tooth smile. She tried to smile in answer but at the last moment she could not open her lips for fear of crying and she bit them instead. Long afterwards he said to her "When you came that first night I thought you'd never smile again. I shall always remember how you looked that night. You looked as if you hadn't any eyes left. You never saw us there."

And then he was saying: "That's Con there. He's the oldest, a year older'n Jedd." The eldest son was in his shirt sleeves, the heavy blue-striped flannel rolled up above his elbows, revealing forearms of fair hairy cord. "Where's your jacket when you come to table?" Wainwright said suddenly. "Can't you put your jacket on when you come to table? Are you in your hot blood? Get your jacket and put it on."

Afterwards the thing she most remembered with significance and sharpness was the fierce flush of blood on the face of the eldest son. It rushed darkly up through his neck and face and seemed finally to bruise the underparts of his eyes and the roots of his thick fair hair. He got up and snatched the jacket from where it hung on a door behind him and Wainwright said:

"Temper, temper. You know what temper does. I'm not ashamed to say what temper did to me. Temper broke my leg for me — that's what it did. And don't mutter at me."

"Who muttered? I never muttered."

"You muttered. I heard you. You muttered under your breath."

"I never muttered. I tell you I never muttered."

"Don't mutter at folks, Con," Mrs. Wainwright said. "Set an example. Eat your supper. I won't have muttering. I won't have people at loggerheads."

It was suddenly dead quiet in the room and Nell said:

"There used to be a family named Wilson up at Top End. Would that be them?"

"Wilton," her father said. "That was their name, Wilton. There were no Wilsons there. Wilton was the name of that family — I know them. I know the folks you mean."

She was only vaguely conscious of listening; she was unaware of whether she was eating or not. Her bread had in fact remained unbroken beside her on the table and now a voice was saying to her, low, in its gentleness almost disembodied:

"Don't you want your bread? I'll eat it if you don't want it."

She shook her head and a moment later Wainwright was saying:

"The only one I didn't tell you about was Matty. He's between Jedd and Nell."

In his shyness, eating her bread, pressing close over his plate, the youngest son did not raise his head to look at her. She heard on all sides the crunch of jaws champing at pickles, the sound of Jedd's lips sucking at dripping vinegar. The powerful smell of the open pickle jar was sour on the air and for nearly a minute there was another sound of Con savagely stabbing with a fork into the heart of the jar, the fork grasped in his hand like a dagger.

"When you've finished, Con, when you've finished," Wainwright said.

"The sergeant says when you've finished," Jedd said.

"Your mother has had nothing. Can't you remember your mother? And what is Matty doing? Matty, whose bread are you eating?"

"Her'n," he said. His voice in its softness seemed almost terrified. "She gin it to me."

"She gin it to me!" Wainwright said. "Gin it! Gin it! What kind of language is that? And sit up! Sit up! Give your mother the pickles."

In this moment of practical righteousness it was Mrs. Wainwright who remembered the bread the girl had never eaten.

"Didn't you want your bread?"

Again she could not bring enough strength to her lips to open them.

"Nor your gruel neither? Don't you want your gruel?"

She felt the crisis of her silence gathering terribly over her as all of them watched her. Once again she could not speak, and with kindness, leaning once more to the side of the lamp, Wainwright said:

"The gruel will do you good. It's good for your chest. If I give you some more hot would you eat it?"

For more than half a minute she could not look up at them; speechlessly she was aware of all the life in her being beaten out.

"You don't have to go out again," Wainwright said. "You can sleep here. Is it that what worries you?"

It was that which worried her; but she could not say it and she shook her head.

"You can sleep with Nell," he said. "She can sleep with Nell, Mother, can't she?"

"We're turning nobody away from here a night like this, that's sure."

"Are you in trouble?" Wainwright said. "I think you're in some trouble, aren't you?"

"Not now."

The words were so low that she could not hear them herself. And for the first time, in a way, she felt that she was not in trouble. There was nothing left of her mind or body or spirit to be in trouble. Her trouble was over. She was sitting at the table as no more than a breath of air contained in a crushed shell, bloodless and thoughtless and incapable of being sick. It was really as if it were the covering shell of death that had grown all about her, screening her chill and her emptiness, and in a way now, at last, it was almost like a comfort.

"Get a brick hot," Mrs. Wainwright said.

Then she was falling. She was falling down the same long wide valley along which she had walked, and on either side of it there were patches of snow that were also faces. It was impossible to separate these faces. Then all at once she knew that they were the same face: the face of Arch Wilson, coming towards her. In her final anguish of fearing to fall and touch it she put out her hands as she had so often done when walking along the valley. They struck the little crowded table in the center. The lamp swayed among the gruel plates. A second later Matty Wainwright leaped forward and caught it with neat quick hands, holding it away, above her head, calm as he turned up the wick for the first time to its full fierce white glow.

I I I

IT was late March before she came downstairs and on into April before she could stand in the narrow yard outside and walk beyond up the thirty or forty feet of ash path towards the row of shops where the shoemakers worked. The house was Number Sixteen of thirty in a row. Beyond the asphalt yards were strips of garden, dark after winter, and then the brick two-storied shops beyond. Primroses, sometimes pink, sometimes with a few green cold daffodils among them, flowered about the paths, splashed by spring rain. Each house possessed a little low iron-wheeled truck and as she came slowly round to herself that spring there were two constant sounds which were really part of her slow waking: the clack of truck wheels running to and from the factories in the streets outside, and the hammering of shoemakers working from daybreak and on into the night, by the light of little tin oil lamps, in the dark-windowed shops all along the row.

It was some time before she became aware of another thing: of how near the river was. She had forgotten that she had come by the river; the days of February and March were lost and clouded. There existed in them only a few light patches of time in which an enormous figure was sitting silently by her bedside, never answering the questions she put to him. "That was Jedd," Mrs. Wainwright told her. "He sat up with you for the rest of his furlough. Jedd could never bear to see nobody suffer."

"Jedd is a good boy," his father said. There was always much talk, especially from Wainwright, of Jedd: a fine pride in the absent one, the soldier. "Always calls me sergeant. Rare boy, Jedd. You can't put Jedd out. I never knowed Jedd put out, not for nobody." There had been a time once, Wainwright said, when a man up at the Quebec Barracks had called him a pug-nosed sod. That was enough to get any man's rag out but Jedd didn't mind. It was water on a duck's back to Jedd. "That's the thing about Jedd. You can't urge him. He never flares up. The day Jedd gets over his collar you'll know summat pretty chronic has happened. Not like Con."

"And where's Jedd now? When will Jedd be home?"

"Jedd's down on the Plain now," they told her. "He'll be home for harvest."

In this way Jedd became, that spring, the almost solitary link between her life as she remembered it before she came down the valley in the snow and the life that began to wake again with the same slow reluctance as the primroses, sooty and rain-beaten, along the many ash paths up and down the yards. She thought distantly, with some sensation of obscure comfort, of Jedd. In her bruised mind she was gradually able to establish Jedd as a bulwark, a wall that would repel and finally obscure with complete extinction the grotesque and terrible pain of her walk in the snow, the death of the baby, the conclusion that there was no Arch Wilson and that now, in fact, there never would be.

For some time the rest of the Wainwrights did not assume the same enlarged bright reality as the figure who was never there. They were pieces of furniture, wooden, set about her in a tidy pattern. It was not until later that she grasped that this was deliberate: that they were withdrawn, wooden and quiet because she could not have borne it otherwise.

In the mornings the men breakfasted and were across the yard, in the shop, before she was up. Then Nell was away, pushing the truck up into the town to fetch uppers from the factory and take the made, finished shoes back again. At half-past twelve they were all in the kitchen again, the men still in their white aprons, the smell of leather strong on their hands, Wainwright always in a curl-brimmed bowler that he took off in the act of sitting down, before grace was said.

On Mondays the copper burned. Some two thousand or so other coppers were burned with it all over the town. The air became thick and acrid, almost rancid, with that odor of burning leather, greasily flaring in copper-holes, that she had first noticed when she had stopped to tie her hair with the piece of bootlace on the road outside the town. The long narrow yard between the houses became something like a shipyard, full of washing that was like flapping, drying sails. On wet days the ceilings of the little kitchens steamed and dripped with washing that could not dry outside, and wet or fine the big clotheshorses stood by the black iron stoves until Tuesday.

On Sundays the men wore clean dickies, starched like curved boards, and narrow hard hats and high, sometimes elastic-sided, black boots that squeaked. There was a silence on the town except for the morning and evening clang of church bells. At eleven, then again at three, and again at six the three men, with Nell and sometimes Mrs. Wainwright, walked to chapel, Mrs. Wainwright in black, Nell in a high-crowned flowering hat. Occasionally Wainwright tramped out into the countryside, to other chapels, to villages from which he returned with proud Methodist rainsoaked fervor or, on fine late spring evenings, with bunches of bluebells or with a sprig of May blossom in his buttonhole. She was not asked to go to chapel. On Sunday mornings she was allowed to sit sometimes by the black Sundaybright stove and beat up eggs, then pale yellow batter, for the Sunday pudding, and the yolky flapping of her slow beating would be the only sound there except the frizzle of beef dripping fat from skewers in a Dutch oven hanging before the fire.

In front of the house was a little parlor, perhaps twelve feet by eight, with a black slate fireplace, the slate scribbled garnet and thrush-egg blue to look like marble, a portrait of William Ewart Gladstone hanging over it; and on another wall two pictures of a golden-bearded Christ in the act of raising the dead and preaching the Sermon on the Mount; and on another sepia portraits of Ben Wainwright at shoemakers' outings, beery and volatile and dandyish in the days before conversion, or on chapel outings, white-dickied, buttonholed and upstanding, in the later purged and beerless years; and then in the wall recesses on either side of the fireplace two cases of butterflies, neat and graduated on pins, from the smallest of feathery blues to large sandy fritillaries and a single big death's-head in the center.

Mrs. Wainwright was proud of the parlor; proud to keep it inviolate; proud of the set of the Nottingham lace curtains and the rose-flecked tea service that came out only at Christmas, the Sunday of the Feast in July and sometimes at Easter time.

She was proud too of her sons: of Matty, the cool, quiet one, of the soldier Jedd, and above all of Con, the first-born. And proudest of all of the butterflies.

"Con was only twelve when he did them," she said. "He bred the death's-head himself. That was the hardest one of all."

Sitting in the window of the parlor, edged forward on a chair, folding back a corner of lace curtain so that she could peer up and down the street outside, she spoke a great deal of Con. Sooner or later something of Con insinuated itself into all her conversation: Con the great one for the river, the meadows and the butterflies, Con the quick-tempered one, Con the one who had to be humored, Con who was the hard one to understand. You had to be patient with Con, firm and patient, she said. His father had never had his measure.

There was something else about Con that brought into her voice and her iron-tipped face a touch of tenderness.

"I had him when I was about your age," she said. "A bit older perhaps. Nineteen."

It was the beginning of a confidence which was really held in exchange for another.

"I fell with Con before I ought to have done," she said. "Like you. I think that's how it was I first knew about you — how you were when you first come here."

"I don't want to talk about that."

"Nell's the only other one that knows. The boys don't know. Even Ben don't know. You needn't worry — I won't tell them neither."

"I don't want to talk about it."

"Was it that Arch Wilson?"

"That was him," she said.

"You're young," Mrs. Wainwright said. "You'll forget it. I know I thought I wouldn't forget it, but I did, in time. You'll forget."

She knew that she never would forget. In a horror that was no less awful now because it was emotionless she looked back and saw some part of herself lying dead in mud and snow and knew that there was no way of forgetting it.

"Like when Ben broke his leg," Mrs. Wainwright said. "That was a terrible time. I thought I wouldn't forget that. Laid up twelve weeks and Jedd away a-soldiering and Matty hardly old enough to run of arrants for me. I made shirts that winter. Sixpence a time. I used to say it was bad when you had to give children bread and scrat, but that winter we never even had bread and scrat. We had good bread though. We always had good bread."

"The leg," she said. "How did he break it?"

"He was drunk."

The girl, not speaking, turned over in her mind the thought of the severe, righteous tramping Wainwright, overinsistent in pride and prayer and decent jackets at supper tables.

"He was drunk and there was a fight and he fell off the high causeway. He was always drunk. I've had him drunk for two weeks. Soaking in it. Then the blues. I seen him fighting lampposts."

She grinned a dry iron smile that did not part her lips.

"I always say that's why he took to the lamplighting. He was sorry for what he'd done to them."

And then, again:

"You're young. We all had trouble. Everybody's had trouble. You have trouble and it's a lesson, like Ben's leg. You've had trouble and you can forget it."

"I forgot it already." She was lying; it was her only defense. "It's gone — I hardly know it's happened."

"I fancy that's the way Ben feels. It's a long time ago. It's gone and he's never been like it again. He used to be hot-blooded, like Con. He's the one that's like him, flaring up, just like Ben was. Matty's like me — cooler."

She grinned again the smile that, between her thin

pursed lips, was hardly a smile at all, but only a cool iron grimace that was kindly.

"I expect that's why I favor Con. He's like his father. They're too much alike — that's why they get at logger-heads."

And then, unexpectedly:

"Perhaps if you stop here you can get work. That'll help you forget. In time you'll meet somebody — is that a portrait of you, upstairs in your drawer?"

"That was me. When I was sixteen."

"When you look like that again you won't have to worry," Mrs. Wainwright said. "They'll be plenty after you again when you look like that."

"I don't want them after me."

"Spring's coming," Mrs. Wainwright said. "It's getting nice by the river now. With the cowslips out. And the cuckoopints. And the cuckoo picking the dirt up. Con would take you down there some time."

Why Con? She had no emotion for Con. Con was a man. She did not want a man. She did not want, ever again, to be taken or touched by a man.

"He's always been the great one for the river," Mrs. Wainwright said. "He'll spend hours there. Days some-times. Roaming the meadows and the back-brooks and watching the pike and things. That's his way — he's funny about things like that. When he gets set on a thing you can't turn him. He'll still go down there, looking for his butterflies and not coming home till he gets them."

The girl wanted to laugh at what seemed the absurd

triviality of a grown man chasing butterflies and she actually gave a smile.

"You can smile," Mrs. Wainwright said. "But you don't know him. You don't know him yet like I do."

I V

IT was not until June that she first walked to the end of the street, seeing the river too for the first time since she had met Wainwright under the street lamps in the melting snow.

As she walked slowly away from the yards and their gray asphalt shade towards the meadows she was always several steps behind Con Wainwright, as if she still had neither strength nor interest to keep up with him. She was dressed in a gray-blue cotton frock, long in the skirt and with a black patent leather belt round the waist, that Nell had found for her and had altered so that it would hang respectably to her thin hipless body. It was the belt, looking not much farther round than the jet necklace Arch Wilson had given her, that was the clue to her terrible thinness. She was wearing too a rather high hat of faded Leghorn straw that Mrs. Wainwright had found and it was too large and pale for the shrunken face that had lost so much of its thick dark crown of hair. She was less than two months from her twentieth birthday but she still looked, that day, like a middle-aged child being led out for con-valescence after illness, to be allowed a first cautious glimpse of the sky.

The only thing that had not changed about her was her way of walking. She still walked with her head up, her neck held rather stiffly, drawn backwards. It was an unconscious habit of pride that had not been crushed and it had the effect, as always, of making her seem taller than she was.

Her first sight of the river at the street-end, where the last houses suddenly plunged down a narrow hill that was blocked at the foot by a gated humpbacked bridge, did not surprise her. She was still not capable of surprise. She saw beyond the bridge, spanned over the deep summer-dark water like a big arching brown-red cat, the beginning of the countryside. Wide meadows repeated themselves, all pasture, far across the valley, to a sky line of spare elms a mile or two beyond. By that time of year all the cattle had been taken from the meadows. The deep flood-silt of winter had fed the grasses so that now the entire valley lay like a vast lake bed of grass, thick and rich, stirring and waving in the sun with soft brushes of pale gold seed.

She stood for some moments on the bridge, side by side with Con Wainwright, and stared at this. Below the bridge, shrouded by chestnut trees, a pub stood above a wooden jetty where occasional barges put in with loads of timber and coal. The blossom of the chestnuts had begun to fall a week or two before; now the last of the pink-white petals were floating down the stream. A few men were sitting on benches under the stone wall of the pub and a woman in a big red-flowered hat sat with white coarse arms bare on the open window sill, the sleeves of her dress rolled up, her mouth downy-white with just the fresh foam of beer as she turned from laughing at someone inside.

At the end of the pub yard, under the chestnuts, two men were playing skittles. She heard the chock of the wooden cheese and the falling skittles without really noticing that it was any different from the blowsy, beery laugh of the woman by the window. She saw that there were four or five boats for hire and she actually noticed the name of one of them, *Jenny,* painted with sign-writer's flourishes on the varnished back of the high cushioned seat inside.

"Would you like to go in a boat or would you rather walk?" he said.

"Whichever you like."

"I can row. We'll have a boat if you'd like to."

"Whichever you like. It makes no difference," she said.

From the window of the pub the woman with the bare arms gave once again her coarse cow-throated laugh. Con Wainwright looked up at her and the sight of her big healthy body filling almost the entire frame of the window made him realize suddenly and acutely how faded and thin the girl beside him was.

"We'll have a boat," he said. "You won't get so tired that way."

Sitting in the boat, staring at Con Wainwright rowing in his shirt sleeves, there was no hint in her mind of any reflection of the moment when she had slid down the riverbank, in the rain, ready to steal a boat because she had some crazy notion of sleeping in it. She was aware of hot evening sun flashing on the smooth surface of the water as the boat drew slowly westward, upstream, and once or twice she shaded her face with the brim of her hat. She was aware of it catching the occasional flat olive plates of water lily leaves or a white wave of moon-daisies thick among the deep grasses in the fields by the river. She was aware of thinking, dully, in a series of mental statements that simply printed themselves on the surface of her mind: "This is nice. The river isn't so wide here. The valley is though. The valley is wide," and in the same flat way she was aware of Con Wainwright talking.

"It gets pretty crowded at the pub summer nights. Everybody gets down there in the summer. You generally get somebody with a fiddle down there and then they start dancing."

When she had no answer to this he said:

"Farther upstream there's a swan's nest. They always build up there. They got five cygnets this year. They had seven last year. That was the most they ever had. If you like we could row up as far as that."

"I don't mind."

"This is Queen's Meadow." He rowed with deliberate slowness, letting the boat glide for a long time between his strokes, trying all the time with desperate interest to wake her so that she at least would become aware, in the hot pure glow of the June evening, of the shape of the country. "That next one is Wyman's Close. And that one over there is Vine Hills. And that's the back-brook over there, other side of the willows. That's where the pike lay."

All this time he was watching her face. Her eyes reminded him of daubs of black lead that his mother put on the stove before it was polished. All the time she sat straight up, head high, in much the same way as she walked, with that terrible frozen hint of unbeaten pride that seemed to indicate that she never wanted to be touched again.

"There's the swans," he said. "All of 'em. See? — just round the bend."

He had turned quickly, picking out the white and gray-brown chain of the birds before she knew where to expect them.

"See 'em?" he said. "That's the old man — him in front, the big one. Then the mother — you can always tell her. She's lower in the water."

Distantly and flatly her eyes accepted the swans exactly as they had accepted the boat, the sun on the water and the great flat lake of silt-fed grass that in a week or two would be one vast map of turning and drying hay. Like all the shoemakers he loved the river. He loved the valley and the open country that was an escape from the low shabby defiles of the town. He felt pride in it because he had been born and bred there and because he knew every pike-hole and every place where bream and roach would be feeding and every spinney and bush and bank where wild duck and snipe and kingfisher would breed. He wanted her to share all this. Already the full surge of summer was rising in the meadow grass, thick-scented, and on the crowns of May blossom and wild rose along the big sprawling hedgerows where later herds of returning cattle would pant flyblown in the August shade, and his pleasure in it made him say:

"You can smell the hedge roses. Smell! Ah! they've all come out today."

"Let's go back," she said.

Afterwards she never knew quite why, at that particular moment, tranquil among the cygnets squeaking after the parent birds and with the scent of wild roses pouring in a sudden light wave of sweetness across the water, she wanted to go back. It was a moment that afterwards reminded her sometimes of the way she had first seen Arch Wilson. It was only the purest chance that had taken her down through the taproom of the Three Bells on the July Saturday evening when she had first seen him there. She had not the slightest business to be in the taproom; she ought to have been turning down the beds in the rooms upstairs; but something had made her slip through the taproom as a short cut to the kitchens at the back. It was a very hot sea-salty day. She had felt a sudden desire for a quick cold drink of water. And as she slipped through the taproom she saw him there for the first time, binding with a spool of dark green thread the tip of a long bream rod he had broken that afternoon on the dykes. As she slipped through from one door to another he looked up at her and she looked back. There was just the hint of a smile on his face and it set her quivering.

"This is where I used to come for butterflies."

He was turning the boat and a moment later the sun, just setting, was out of her eyes. She saw him pointing to a long sloping bank thick with scarlet and yellow vetch and crowned with pink-brown bushes of fading may.

"July," he said. "July and August. Clouds of them. Sometimes you'd think the bank was dancing or else on fire."

Again she wanted to laugh at the apparently trivial notion of a man chasing butterflies. She actually smiled again as she had done when she had first heard it from his mother. In the tender afterglow of sunset his face was dreamy and he said:

"One day I'll bring you up here. You can see for yourself then. About a month from now. July."

In rapidly softening twilight they landed at the jetty, under the chestnut trees, about half an hour later. He had rowed back rather faster with the flow of the stream. There were lights in the pub by this time but outside it was still light enough to see the color of women's dresses as they sat drinking on the benches.

He had finished tying up the boat and was feeling in his pocket for the shilling to pay for it when he turned suddenly and saw her staring up towards the windows of the pub with a look of almost idiot astonishment. Under the too-large hat her face had exactly the compressed and vacant look, partly terrified, of a person trapped in a moment of lunacy.

At the same moment she put out her hands exactly as she had done so many times when walking along the valley. She began trembling and he heard her shudder.

"That's Arch Wilson," she said. He heard her voice stuttering between her half-clenched teeth. "That's Arch Wilson up there."

"Where? Which one? Arch Wilson — who's he?"

Before she had time to say anything he remembered. He recalled the night of her arrival, out of the February darkness: the white crushed figure brought in from the street by his father.

"You don't recollect any Arch Wilson here, do you, Jedd?" he remembered his father saying and then Jedd answering "No, sergeant" and the terrible sightless look on her face as she listened, knowing that nobody had heard of Wilson and looking as if, at last, she was coming to realize that nobody ever would.

"Which one? Which one is he?"

"The one with the fair mustache. The big one. The one under the window."

She was still staring up the slope of the yard with her look of idiot vacancy. In the twilight her face seemed to have shrunk still more under the wide stiff hat. He remembered saying "Is that him you wanted to find when you first come here?" and then the blood started pounding heavily, in enormous waves, up through his throat.

He did not remember much after that. He was partly aware of rushing up the slope, wiping the back of one hand across his face in a first huge muscular gesture of anger.

Then he was saying: "Mister, there's a lady wants to speak to you. She's down there, mister — she wants you."

The man was sitting on a bench, cross-legged, with a mug of beer in one hand and a straw hat balanced on the tip of his knee.

Nervously his fingers plucked at the band of the hat.

"What lady? Where? I don't know any lady —"

"You got eyes in your head, ain't you? Down there — by the boat."

"I don't know her. I don't know nobody here —"

"Look, shopmate" — he was standing over him, menacing, unaware of much except the trembling straw hat and the level of the beer squalling over as the glass was set down on the bench — "she wants a word with you. She's been looking a long time for you."

"I don't come from here. I don't know nobody here. I'm from Bedford — I come from Bedford. I got folks here —"

"Get up, Wilson," he said. His rage was concentrated on the dangling, trembling straw hat and he did not hear anything of the answer: "I ain't Wilson. My name ain't Wilson —"

"Come on — talk to her!" he yelled.

A moment later he had the man by the collar, wrenching him to his feet. The straw hat was bouncing down the yard. The big woman on the other side of the window started shouting "Fight! Fight! Somebody's fighting!" and the man began striking out wildly with both hands. In the struggle, as he bent to pick up his hat, his big silver watch suddenly spewed itself from his waistcoat pocket. It swung to and fro like a pendulum across his belly. He staggered about, trying to catch it, shouting:

"My watch! My watch! Don't break my watch —"

"I'll break your damn' neck! Come on — don't whine so

much. You know her — she's Bella. She wants to speak to you."

"Bella?" Desperately he grabbed his watch at last, clutching it like a ball. "Bella? I don't know nobody named Bella — "

"Down there! Take and look at her. There she is — now make out you don't know her."

By that time she had walked slowly up from under the deeper twilight cast by the chestnut trees. Perhaps out of distraction, perhaps with the idea of making her face clearer and more recognizable to Wilson, she had taken off her hat.

Then as he came down the slope she suddenly stood still, watching him. With trembling fingers he was trying to put the watch back into his waistcoat pocket and now, slippery and silver, it kept dancing like a fish on the chain. All the time he was not so much concerned with her as with the watch. Then suddenly the big woman yelled from the window of the pub:

"His name ain't Wilson. It's Faulkner. Harry Faulkner — "

"That's right, that's right," he said. "Faulkner, Faulkner — "

Her face was dead white in the summer darkness.

"You wanta be more careful, limbing folks about!" the woman yelled. "You'd get one across the chops an' quick, limbing some folks about — "

"Is this him?" Con said.

The collar the man was wearing was of a kind of patent

paper, white, turned down, that could be worn once or twice and thrown away. The clip-tie had become loose from underneath it. It was dropping down as if from a crushed paper bag.

Breathing hard, holding his hands across his watch, retrieved now, caught at last and stuffed back into his pocket, the man said:

"I git heart attacks if I ain't careful. I ain't Wilson. My name's Faulkner — I never seed her before."

"Is this him, Bella?"

"I git heart attacks — " he was panting, holding his watch pocket, mouth loosely open, convulsing.

"Is it him?"

She did not answer. He knew there was no need to answer. The expression on her face had changed. He actually saw the thin muscles of it tightening in the light from the windows of the pub. She seemed to be looking not only at and into the face of the fleshy panting Faulkner but round it and beyond it, as if making quite sure that it was not Arch Wilson, cheating her after all.

Something about this look seemed to unnerve him more than anything that had happened before and he said:

"I ain't nobody you know, am I? God's truth, I ain't, am I?"

"No," she said. Speaking to him for the first time, she was not bitter. What she said was like a warning, coldly even and steady. "No, but you could have been."

"See? — you could have been," Con said, "couldn't

you? Git back where you spring from. Git back to Bedford."

"I got a right to go where I like." Desperately he was
trying now to refix the torn paper collar about his neck.
"You wanta keep your hands off folks — one o' these
days you'll do it once too much. You'll do it once too
much."

"Ah! Go home!" the big woman yelled. "All of you!"

"This is a rough town," the man said. "Everybody knows
that. It's always been rough. You can't come into this
town 'ithout somebody starts fighting. That's shoemakers
all over — fighting, don't wanta let nobody else live,
always fighting — "

"Come on, Bella," Con said.

He took her by the arm. He felt the flesh of it stiff and
thin as an ash rod.

"Don't wanta let nobody else live, do you? That's shoemakers all over, that is, that's shoemakers — " The voice
whined and repeated itself and dropped away in the windless summer darkness.

It was not until they were almost at the top of the hill
that Con stopped and turned and spoke to her.

"Who was he? Wilson?"

"A man I knew."

"What'd he do to you?"

"Nothing. Nothing. It was nothing."

"You want to see him again?"

"No," she said. "Not now. Not any more."

Some time later they were standing by a fence, under the

last unlaid arch of a hawthorn hedge before the fences of the town began. The scent of fading blossom was warm and drowsy on the night air. Beyond the hedge a field of wheat was rising into ear. He heard the faintest stir of wind walking with a rustle across the dry young beards.

"I'd be jealous if you wanted him." All the hot spurt of his temper had died. He hardly knew, now, what he had done or said in the first few blinding moments above the nervous straw hat.

"Jealous?"

She lifted her face. He saw her mouth actually break into a smile, her teeth shining, and she said:

"You got mad, didn't you?"

"A bit."

"You often get mad like that?"

"When anything urges me."

She smiled again. Suddenly he felt that she looked so transfigured by it that he put one arm completely round her, holding her against him.

"Bella," he said. "Bella."

A moment later he was trying clumsily to kiss her. She ducked her head sharply. There was nothing in front of his lips but the dark thinned crown of her hair and with amazement he heard her crying into her hands.

He let her cry for some time longer simply because he did not know what to say or do that would stop it except that once or twice he put his mouth against her hair.

"Would you come out with me?" That was all he could say. It was a long time afterwards when he thought he heard the footsteps of people walking up the hillside from the pub below.

"Yes," she said. "I'll come out with you."

As she lifted her face, not crying now, he tried to kiss it again but for the second time she held it away, not ducking, but drawing her head back from him instead.

"Can't I kiss you?"

"Not yet. Not now."

"Don't you want me to kiss you?"

"Not now. Not so soon."

Walking up the hill again, holding her narrow waist almost with the span of one hand, he heard the wind once more walking with its delicate prolonged rustle across the young ears of wheat. The sound, like a long receding sigh, touched into complete wakefulness the nerves of his own sensations. The wheat too reminded him of something else.

"You'd never think the summer could go so fast," he said. "It'll soon be harvest," and as he spoke he heard her, with fresh amazement, giving a dry short laugh.

"What are you laughing at?" he said.

"I was thinking of you," she said, "and how mad you were."

A few minutes later, at the top of the street, they came to Mrs. Wainwright waiting under the lamp that stood at the end of the row.

"Is that you, Con?" she said. "I was waiting for your father." Every night, at eleven o'clock, Wainwright hustled limping through the town, putting out the street lamps. "Did you have a nice time? Did you both enjoy yourselves?"

"Mother," he said. "Bella's going to come out with me."

"Is she? That's nice," she said. She peered with the faintest air of anxiety up the street. "I don't see your father. Where's he got to?" She made the smallest vexatious pursing movement of her lips: it might have been that she was afraid that one night, some time or other, Wainwright would not come home.

"I'll step as far as the top and meet him," she said. Her lips relaxed for a second in the fondness of her gaze at Con, her glance up and down the dress the girl was wearing was almost tender. "I like you in that dress. Don't you think it looks nice on her, Con?"

"I like it," he said.

"You go in now," she said. "You'll just have time to undress by the street light, Bella, if you want to."

Upstairs, in the small front bedroom where the two girls slept together, she did as Mrs. Wainwright said. Slowly, in the green light of the lamp that did not go out till nearly forty minutes later, she undressed and put on the big flannel nightgown that, like all her clothes, was something Nell had found for her. She stood by the window for a long time looking out, hearing the footsteps of Mrs. Wainwright pacing on the asphalt below.

"Aren't you coming to bed?" Nell said. "Aren't you sleepy?"

"I didn't want to wake you."

"I haven't been to sleep. It's too hot. I've been wondering where you were."

"We had a boat on the river."

Almost unconsciously she stood drawing her hands up and down the flanks of her body. She could feel the straight hard bones of her thighs and the stony edges of her hips, both graceless, almost without flesh. Through the open upper sash of the window the night air of late June was still and hot, without wind, and from somewhere, delicately, was borne the first scent of hay. She did not know how long she breathed this scent without noticing it. It might have been for ten minutes or so. Then she was not only aware of it but she was aware of it waking her. She began to recall, because of it, the way she had let herself be rowed on the river. She remembered the swans, the huge white pools of daisies starry in high meadow grass, the rise and fall of fish and the immense hot afterglow of midsummer on the far westerly crest of the valley. She had forgotten that there were such things.

For most of the time, as she stood there, Nell talked from the bed:

"Did you like it with Con? Did you get on all right together?"

"I think so. He wants me to go out with him."

"And will you? That'll be nice for you."

"I think so."

"And for him too." Nell was lying with her bare plump arms outside the coverlet, her fair hair plaited, each rope of it down on her shoulders, tied with a white night ribbon. "He's been out with girls before but somehow it never lasts long."

"Perhaps they urge him to death."

Nell laughed. "I'll bet he said that to you, didn't he? That's the way he talks."

"Yes: that's what he said to me."

She stood by the window for a few minutes longer, the street light still not out, Wainwright still not home, her hands still making the partly conscious exploration of the thin hard sides of her body. For some time there was not even the sound of Mrs. Wainwright's footsteps pacing the asphalt and then Nell said:

"Are you coming into bed now? It must be going up hill for twelve."

"I was just wondering where your father was — why he wasn't in."

"Oh! he'll come. Mother always whittles about him but sometimes he gets a lamp that won't go out. I never worry, though." She laughed from the bed.

The light of the street lamp was still not out when Bella lay down in the tiny stifling room, in the small iron bedstead where there was hardly room for the two of them to lie without touching. "It's a good job we're both not fat," Nell said and as she moved to throw back the second of the top sheets her body, too plump, moist in the restless heat, swung against the body of the other girl, bony, rigid, so fined down that it was still almost as straight as the body of a boy.

"Are you excited?"

"Why?"

"Going out with Con. I should be excited."

She did not answer. She lay staring at the ceiling,

green in the light of the lamp. She wondered if it was possible, ever again, to feel excited. The bars of the window made a hard and brilliant shadow on the ceiling and as she lay watching it she saw herself clearly, for the first time for four or five months, free from the complex veil of distances that had separated her from the time when she had been lying in another room, on another summer night; when she too, like Nell, had not been able to sleep because it was too hot and she was too excited.

She remembered how anxious and trembling and full of wonder she had been. She remembered how terribly proud she had been of her young full breasts, rosy-brown in the candlelight, and the graceful way her long candle-gold flanks had curved like a harp in the bed.

"I hate you. I'll always hate you. I hate you. I'll go on hating you."

She remembered her desperate illusion that the man by the river had been Arch Wilson. She recalled a single stunned moment when she would have been glad if Con, raging blindly up the yard under the chestnut trees, had killed him as he sat there.

"As long as I live I know I'll hate you."

"What did you say?"

"Nothing." Her lips were trembling. In distress she had been unaware of speaking aloud. "Nothing."

"I thought you'd gone to sleep. I thought you were talking in your sleep."

"No. No, I wasn't talking."

"You talk in your sleep sometimes," Nell said. "You

shout out. When you were first here you used to sit up and start screaming and I had to hold you down."

She had nothing to say to that; she was not surprised by that. What surprised her, as she lay stiffly in the hot bed, watching the cross on the ceiling, was the strength of her hatred against Arch Wilson. She had not been prepared for that.

A little later the light of the street lamp went out. The dark cross vanished suddenly and she knew that Wainwright was home.

As the summer went on, mostly dry, sometimes with deep sultry storm-heavy nights when the air was crushed between the low walls of the valley and breathlessly between the walls of the little house, she walked out with Con. Formally, arm in arm, they walked through the streets of the town, along the towpath by the river, across meadows from which by July all the great silt-fed crop of hay had been carted and to which the cattle had returned.

She did not think of this as a courtship. It was not possible to feel that it was any more than a sort of exercise. It was a phase, like that of learning to play the piano, where a series of formal exercises of humdrum repetition were the preparation for something that was perhaps to be, in time, more rewarding and more beautiful.

Presently there were signs of changes in her. Her body began to fill out again and her face had color. Her hair, a dull black lead, opaque, without luster, exactly like her eyes, began to grow again and sometimes she gave it

brushings of Macassar oil to make it shine. She began to
show not merely the unconscious pride that had always
made her walk so erectly, but a pride in which there was
thought and preparation. She began to stand by the mirror again, up in the little bedroom she shared with Nell,
trying on perhaps the changed collar of a dress, looking
at herself in the jet necklace Arch Wilson had given her,
pushing the curl of her black hair away from her ears.
She had small delicate ears, rather narrow and pointed,
and when she pushed the hair away from them they
glowed china-white under the blackness of it, like neat
suspended shells. Once when she looked at them she
remembered that she had always wanted earrings. "I'm
dark," she thought. "Earrings would suit me. Not gold
ones. Perhaps pearl ones. Those with pearl drops." Out
of this thought for the future she actually achieved a
new attitude about the past. She took out the photograph of herself that had been taken when she was sixteen and looked at it with something more than a search
of pride. With hesitant affection she compared the face
there with the face of herself as she saw it now.

"You're getting a bit more like it," she thought. "You
were fatter in the face then. But your hair's the same.
That's come back. That's all right again."

In this way she thought, for the first time, of her shoes.
Up to July she had managed with the old high-legged
laced-up boots of black calf that had so shocked Wainwright when he first saw them, plastered with the sludder
of melted snow; or she had put on a pair of Nell's. But

[59]

now she remembered the shoes Arch Wilson had given her and she took them out again. She had never worn them before. They had always been, she thought, like ornaments that were too good, too beautiful and too precious to wear.

"I might wear them for Sundays," she thought.

Then when she tried them on for the first time she found that her feet, like the rest of her body, had lost flesh and were smaller. The shoes slopped loosely up and down. But then as she stood with them in her hands, disappointed, wondering what to do, Nell came into the bedroom.

"Oh! that's easy," Nell said. "Dad'll do that, or Con or one of them. You want a thin sock in them, that's all."

"Would they? You think one of them could do them now?"

"You could go over to the shop and see," Nell said. "I know Dad's not there. Nor Con. Con's getting ready. But Matty might be there."

"I'll go and see."

"The only thing is they might take some time to dry."

"That won't matter," she said. "Con will always wait for me."

She walked across the yard, down through the narrow garden, where a few neat rows of onions and carrots and summer lettuce and a fringe of yellow nasturtiums brightened the cracking clay, and then on to the shop. She had never been there before. The cramped two-storied building had a grease-soaked flight of wooden steps going up to the second floor. She stood on the bottom step and called up to find if anyone was there. The door at the top of the stairs was closed but it opened almost immediately and Matty appeared.

"Nell said you might do something for me," she said. "Shall I come up?"

"Oh! yes, come up," he said. "Come up."

He stood holding the door open, collarless, sleeves up, his arms black to the elbows with the stain from a boot he had been finishing and which he was still holding in one hand.

"Yes, come up. Come in," he said. It did not strike her until long afterwards how many times he repeated the words. "Come up. Come in. You've never been up here before."

"No," she said. She stood looking round the small oblong whitewashed shop, with its crowded benches under the cobwebbed leather-dusted windows; the rolls of kip and calf and belly-leather and the untidy mess of tins and sprigs and eyelets and brass tacks and wax end. A glue pot was cooling on its burner. She could smell the hot breath of it and with it the close dark odor, almost the stench, of leather.

Very often afterwards she remembered how he took the shoes in his hands and how he dropped one of them as he turned them over. He was several inches shorter than either Con or Jedd and there was a shyness about his pale, exceptionally fair eyes that made him seem, sometimes, a trifle shortsighted.

[61]

It seemed for some moments as if he were peering through the shoes, microscopically dissecting them. He ran his fingers once or twice across the stitching and then along the inside linings, about the toe.

"Where'd you get shoes like this?"

"I had them when I came here," she said. "I had them given to me."

His fair pale eyes, with their impression of shortsightedness, were too shy to look at her face. They seemed to look down through the uppers of the shoes and then through the soles of the shoes at her feet instead.

"You don't want to wear shoes like this. Not you."

"Why? Why not?" she said.

"They're muck," he said. "Cheap muck. That's all they are."

"Cheap?"

"Look at the linings," he said. "Like paper. Look at the buckles."

She remembered her first great wonder at the beauty of the buckles, how smart they were, how silvery and how exciting.

"They get some muck up nowadays," he said. "What d'ye suppose would happen if you got out in the rain?"

"I know they don't fit me," she said, "but they'd do, wouldn't they, if you put socks in? They're all I got."

"I could put socks in," he said.

As he found a pair of socks and began to trim them to

size with his knife she found herself watching his hands. She had never noticed the hands of Arch Wilson or Con or anyone else as she now noticed the hands cutting and sticking and pressing the socks into her shoes. They were very small hands; and as she watched them she forgot that her shoes were cheap; she even forgot the effect of her painfully destroyed illusion that the buckles were wonderful things. She stood fascinated by a marvelous neatness in the short, well-shaped fingers, a bony delicacy that reminded her of the toes of a bird. She saw that he could put almost the entire hand into the toe of the shoe and lose it there.

Presently her astonishment at the hands was the only thing left in her mind. It was something she could no longer keep quiet about and she said:

"You've got such small hands. I can't help noticing them. They're no bigger than mine."

He held them up, smiling for the first time.

"Didn't you ever notice them before?"

"No. I didn't notice them."

"I made the smallest pair of shoes in England once," he said. He spoke with shy pride, rubbing each thumb along the tips of his fingers. "I was the only one who could do it. They were no bigger than this." He pressed three of his fingers together. "No bigger than a bean pod. They were for a little midget. On the halls in London. A dancer."

"I never saw a man with such small hands," she said. Suddenly she was putting her own hands flatly against his, left against right, right against left, the fingers outspread.

"The same size," she said.

He did not speak. She could feel the tips of her fingers tingling with minute pulses of blood that woke exact responses in his, like the tick of two small clocks put face to face, close together.

"It's funny," she said, "a man with such small hands." She found herself wanting to let the minute fascinating beat of the two pairs of fingers go on a little longer, and then suddenly she felt touched by his own shyness, exactly as if it were pouring into her through the tiny pulses of his fingers.

She gave a small laugh and drew her hands away. Not at that moment, but later, she experienced an odd sensation that for the first time in her life she was really aware of her hands. As she lay in bed that night she lifted her hands above the sheets and spread out the five fingers of each and pressed them against the darkness. She felt the air of the summer night floating delicately through them with velvet breath. And as she did so she re-experienced the sensation of the pulsing finger tips pressed against her own with minute beats of communication and she could hear Matty saying again:

"If you really want a pair of shoes I'll make you a pair."

"You? Would you?"

Nobody in this town reckons to make women's shoes," he said. "Con and Jedd and Dad — they never bin much cop at it. But I could make a pair. I do all the things like that — special pairs. Fancy things — shoes for dancers. Would you let me make you a pair?"

"If you would," she said. "I should like it if you would."

"I'll measure you now if you like," he said. "While you're here."

She felt an odd sensation of uncertainty, not quite nervousness, as he said this.

"I got to go now," she said. "I don't want to keep Con waiting."

"All right, tomorrow then?" She heard him in a slightly confused way telling her how, at nights, he liked staying on in the shop, when it was quieter, after the rest had gone, working on, finishing things. "Con — he's the one for walking and the river and all that. But I like it up here. By myself," he said.

"Shall I come in then tomorrow?"

"Yes," he said. "And think if there's anything you'd like on them. Buckles or anything."

"I think I'd like buckles," she said.

"Have anything you like. Anything," he said.

That evening as she walked out with Con through footpaths cut through wheatfields that were now as high as her shoulders and paling already with the first olive-blue flush before ripening, it did not occur to her to speak of the shoes. It was something that she wanted to keep, like the sensation of pressing her fingers against those of his incredibly small hands, absolutely to herself.

It was something secretive, simple and yet not explicable, that she did not want to share.

As they walked back across the fields, under a sky of unbroken sultry cloud, a slight rain began to fall. It was hardly more, at first, than a summer night mist drawn up from the river and sown on the heavy July wind. She felt it settling finely on her face and hair. Then presently it was falling fast enough for Con to say "We'd better shelter for a minute. Get underneath a tree." Far off, across the cornfields, she could see constant flashes of summer lightning. Great pale yellow sheets pounded at the sky like signals and once, under a nearer larger flash, she saw the entire cornfield before her flare into life, green-white, a sea of pointed ears.

"Only another fortnight," Con said, "and we'll start harvesting."

She was not really listening. She knew that in August the whole town shut down its shops. Whole families came out into the fields and reaped and tied and harvested, working from daybreak to dark. For a month there was no more shoemaking. After that, in September, when the wagons had emptied the fields, the women stayed on for gleaning, taking home vast bundles of wheat and barley. "I recollect we had enough to thresh one year," Mrs. Wainwright had told her. "A good-sized stack. That was when Con and Jedd and Matty were boys, afore they started to use a scythe. You should see Con with a scythe. And Jedd too. The way they rip into it, Con especially, — you'd think they were murdering the corn."

Above her, in the oak tree, she heard a sudden patter of heavier raindrops on the thick dark leaves. She was surprised into lifting her face. Then a flash of lightning lit up, a second later, all the leaves and branches and the thick fissured bark of the trunk against which she was leaning. Then she felt her face pressed back, hard and sharp on the bark, and Con was kissing her.

"No," she said. "No."

"You never kissed me all the time we bin out together," he said.

"I told you, I don't want to be kissed. I told you."

"All summer and you never kissed me. Not once. Not so much as —"

"I told you," she said. "I told you when we started. That first time."

"That was different. That was weeks ago."

"It's no different now," she said. "I don't want it to be different."

"Don't walk on!" he said. "It's raining faster. You'll get wet —"

But already she was walking on. And then he was following, almost at a run, slashing suddenly at the heads of cornstalks with the ashplant he was carrying.

"What's the matter with you? Don't you ever kiss anybody?"

She did not answer. There was no need to answer and he said:

"All we do is just walk. Walk and walk and walk." His voice had a locked, constricted, goaded sound. "You don't want me, do you? That's about the drift on it — you don't want me."

Before she could answer he caught her by the tips of her narrow shoulders. His hands were so large that his finger tips almost met her back. She threw up her head in a quick agonized little gesture of pain that seemed to enrage him and he said:

"Don't urge me. Don't toss your head like that — "

"I don't like men who hurt me," she said. "I don't want to be hurt."

"Men?" he said. "What men? Did you ever have men before you were here?"

"Let me go now," she said.

"What men were you talking about?"

"Nobody. Nothing. I'm tired. I want to go — "

"I don't like being made a fool on," he said. "I don't stand for that. That's what I don't stand for — "

She broke away at last. He followed her, tramping heavily up the footpath, not speaking again until they reached the stile at the end of the field. It was raining fast by that time. She could hear soft sheets of it, wind-driven, hissing through the corn.

"Wait a minute, wait a minute," he said.

He ran several paces ahead of her, reaching the stile a moment before she did. He leaped over it and stood on the other side. All summer, in just that way, in the simple formal country fashion, he had climbed stiles and fences so that he could help her down the other side. He had not grasped that it was a demonstration of something she had needed much more than kisses. It was beyond him to know that what he had done in that simple way had done so much to restore in her the things that had been shattered.

"I didn't mean that," he said. "I never meant to talk like that."

She could not see his face very clearly in the darkness; but all the expression of it, big, groping, drained of anger, was clear in his way of speaking. She heard the rain rustle harder in the corn. Then a great burst of sheet lightning lit up dramatically the white bars of slanting rain, his face and his upstretched hands.

"It's all right," she said. "I know how you feel. I do know. But — well, some day, soon perhaps — "

That was all she could say. His hands spanned her waist and lifted her down. The warm rain on the dry dust of the road beyond the field had made the air smell sweetly. She thought of how little she wanted to quarrel with anyone and how much she needed quietness. And then suddenly the rain made a final unexpected hiss across the corn, rushing back across the dark fields like frightened feet. A sheet of lightning flapped low in the sky and in the white-yellow light of it she saw his hands enormously outspread, palms upward, in the rainless air.

"It's left off. It's all finished," he said. Every trace of anger in his voice had gone. He was once again the man who had lifted her over a hundred stiles, bringing to her a tenderness he had no other way of expressing. "If we'd waited a bit we wouldn't have got wet."

She wanted to say "That was me. That was all my fault," but she did not say it. She was thinking instead of Matty's hands: how extraordinary and delicate and feminine they were in their smallness, so well-shaped and capable and expressive, exactly the same size as her own. She was thinking — perhaps not thinking so much as wondering, balanced somewhere between reflection and surprise — how strange it was that she had not noticed them before, and how still more strange was the sensation of the fingers ticking with their tiny pulses of blood in time with her own.

She was quick to notice them again the following evening when she climbed the steps of the shop. Hearing the latch of the downstairs door, he was already at the head of the stairs, waiting for her. His hands were holding a stabbing awl. And she noticed how delicately he held it, with a kind of poised lightness, as a doctor holds a probe.

Then as she sat down — he had borrowed one of the kitchen chairs for her and he himself sat in front of her on a three-legged stool about nine inches high — she remembered something else. She remembered some words of Arch Wilson's:

"Threes. Narrow fitting. No bigger than a doll's."

A moment or two later, as she watched him draw round the shape of her foot with pale blue chalk on a sheet of gray-brown pattern paper, she knew that that was another lie.

"I should say you're threes and a half," he said. "Perhaps a bit more."

"I always thought I was threes," she said. "That's what they always said."

"Threes would kill you," he said.

He held one of her feet in his hands and she remembered the excited sensation of Arch Wilson also holding them, the sea wind cool on her stockinged soles in the bristling fen-land afternoon. Now the sensation was warmer, quieter, altogether more soothing than that had been.

"It's not the size so much," he said. "You're high in the instep — here." His fingers curved across the arch of her foot. "That's what makes you walk like you do." He was smiling. "You walk on your toes, don't you?"

"I don't know. I never noticed."

"Hardly anyone knows how they walk," he said. "You walk straight up. That's through walking on your toes."

For a moment she did not know what to say. Something made her recall the malty, smoothing way Arch Wilson would have said a thing like that — "Walking on your toes, never knew that, did you? But I did, didn't I — I tell you, I'm a shoemaker. That's how I noticed" — but there was no single hint in Matty's voice of anything remotely like that smooth, thick pride.

"When did you first notice I walked like that?"

"That night," he said, "when you come home with Dad. You were done in, but that's how you were walking."

[71]

She did not say anything. Queer, she thought, how if it hadn't been for shoes I wouldn't have been here in the first place. And then with amazement she heard him say:

"I thought we'd have to cut your boots off. Your feet were so swollen. You couldn't have had your boots off for days."

"Somebody cleaned them up nice," she said, "and half-soled and heeled them. I know that. Was that you?"

"Yes," he said.

He got up rather suddenly, with some shyness, and laid the pattern paper on the bench. At the same time he lifted and set aside the little stool. She was fascinated by the stool. The yellow grain of its worn pine seat looked like the arrow-bones of a fish-back. He saw that she was fascinated and said:

"Dad made that. I couldn't reach the bench when I first started up here and he made that for me to stand on. Most boys have a box at first."

"When did you first start?"

"I was seven and in my eight," he said. "I used to go and stand by the window over there and stare down the valley and wish I was somewhere." He was smiling again: the same withdrawn, self-effacing smile, the fair white-blue eyes averted. "I do now, come to that. I never wanted to be up here. I hated it up here."

He walked over to the small north-facing window and rubbed a dusty cobweb or two from the face of the glass with his hand.

"Can you see the white thing on the hill across there?

— above the spinney?" She picked out from the summer hedges on the slope of the valley a spike of something white. "That's Stone Cross," he said. "I got as far as that once. All my things in a sprig-bag. Half a quartern loaf and two onions and a shoe-knife. I got it into my head that that was London — just over yonder. Over the hill."

With a quick flick of his hands he brushed at another cobweb. As he did so a spider rushed from the dust-clogged corner of the pane and then stopped, dead-poised, in the center. She watched it without speaking, thinking, again perhaps not so much thinking as reflecting with a sort of slow surprise: "Someone else, then, knows what it's like to start off by yourself. Going somewhere. Alone. All your things in a bag."

"How often did you feel like that?"

"About every day at first. Not quite so much later."

"Watch the spider go back if I touch the web," she said.

She held her finger over the strands of the web and the spider seemed to watch her.

"Still, I don't have to walk to London now if I go," he said. "That's one blessing. I got enough to ride with now."

"London?" She was so surprised that her finger brushed the web before she was aware of it. She saw the dark bag of the spider scurrying past her hand. "You still want to go there? That isn't the place for you."

"Why not?"

"I couldn't see you there somehow," she began to say, but he said quickly:

"You've never been in Nenweald in a bad winter, have you?"

"Your mother told me about it. About how — "

"Bread and scrat, that's what they live on. The kids on barley-pap. Everybody at the pop shop. Nothing even to get drunk with. I seen as many as seventy or eighty houses empty and not a shop working. Folks moonlight-flitting every night and young chaps off on tramp, workhouse to workhouse. That's the sort of winter we get every once in a while. We're about due for one now — we ain't had one lately."

He laughed and said that was how Queenie Foster found out about the asylum. Queenie Foster, a pink, pig-necked woman of forty who lived at the end of the row, hair curl-ragged from Sunday to Sunday, belly wrapped in a sack-apron, let her back bedrooms to male lodgers whose children she could not feed. She lolled about the yards, borrowing salt, begging pinches of baking powder. "Ain't got a mite o' salt, gal, ayer? I'll gin y' it back, gal, soon's I bin up-street. But I got Solly a-bed, gal, I got Solly a-bed again." Mr. Foster loafed sadly about the kennel of a house like a drawn whippet, blue-lipped, shaking under a palsied, pallid skin. For years Queenie got drunk every Saturday and fought the lampposts; but now, every six weeks or so, a black closed cab came down the yards and Queenie went away.

"She first did that seven or eight years ago. Had a blind

on her harvest money that lasted three weeks. Nobody could do nothing with her. Then they took her away and she liked it. So now she goes regular — it's nice in there."

"Hadn't you better come and get your supper?"

He smiled. He said he was sorry he had talked so much. He was too shy to tell her how much he had liked it and some of his shyness spread suddenly to her in a curious wave of feeling that made her guiltily remember Con.

"Con'll wonder where I am. What time is it? How long have I been here?"

From under the bib of his shoemaker's apron he drew out his watch. It was a small neat watch, silver, on a leather strap.

"It's going up hill for seven." He saw her, as he thought, looking at the watch, though in reality she was looking at the hand which held it, thinking how like him it was to choose a watch that was no larger than a crown-piece.

"It's a nice watch," he said. "I got it at Bedford. I went over by train and got it. I had my name put in." He flicked open the back of the watch and showed her his name, "Matthew George Wainwright," engraved on the mirroring silver inside.

"You're lucky you can afford a watch like that," she said.

"It repeats too." He pressed the lever. She heard the tiny chimes repeating themselves, all the silence of the shop compressed and contracted as they died away. "I saved up for it. When I want something I save up for it."

She felt him to be suddenly amazingly sure of himself.
The ticks of the watch started minute echoes in her finger
tips. He put the watch back in his waistcoat pocket and
then took out from his trouser pocket a leather key-bag.
"I made that." He pulled his apron over his head and
hung it on the door-nail. "I like things neat and tidy."
Three keys, one for his watch, one of brass and slightly
larger, another of steel, fitted into the brown oval bag
with the neatness of seeds in a pod.

He held up the brass key. "That's for my worldly
wealth. I got that in Bedford too." Then, in a last short
rush of words, as if all the time he had been leading up
to it and had never quite dared: "I go over there once
every few weeks. It's a big town, good shops there. That's
where I'll get your buckles."

When they went in to supper the rest of the Wainwrights were already eating. Between violent purple
mouthfuls of beetroot Wainwright said:

"Here you are, seem'ly. Couldn't think where you'd got
to."

"Matty's going to make me a pair of shoes," she said.
"We've been — "

"Shoes? What shoes?" She saw Con, flushed, stabbing
at a flaring moon of beetroot, looking up. "I thought
you'd got shoes."

"Not as she can wear," Matty said.

"Who said so?"

"All she's got is threes. And threes would kill her."

"So you're going to make a pair. Mister Paul Pry is

going to make a pair. Nosey's going to make a pair —"

"Any more o' that and you'll feel the back of my hand across your mouth!" Wainwright said. "I won't have that!"

"Skinflint," Con said. "I wonder he don't shave the hair off his face and save that."

"I won't have that sort of talk!" Wainwright said. "You can put a sock in that!"

"Let him put a sock in it."

"Don't mutter at me!" Wainwright said. "I'll make you mutter the other side of your face, I warrant. I'll make you mutter."

"I got something to mutter about —"

"Then outside! Outside!" Wainwright struck the table a terrible blow with the handle of his knife, so that the purple blood of the beetroot quivered and spattered. "Not here! I won't have it here! Not at the table! — not here!"

"Then let him keep his nose out. Tell him —"

"Tell him! What business is it of mine to tell him? Who am I to tell what he shall do and what he shan't do? If Matty wants to make her shoes let him make her shoes."

"It's her birthday," Matty said.

"Birthday? Who said it was her birthday? When?"

"That's when!"

Across the little table Mrs. Wainwright reached with pouncing swiftness and hit him full across the face with the flat of her hand, a quick crackling blow of David and

Goliath that did not rouse him to a single word in answer. He sat glowering at the center of the table, blood-flushed, afraid of her, eyes terribly dark, hands out of sight.

"I will not have you at loggerheads," she said. "You know I will not have you at loggerheads."

His hands were revealed, pushing away his plate.

"And eat your food. Don't we work hard enough to get the food?"

Wainwright raised his eyes to the cracked low ceiling and there was not a sound in the room.

"And now let's have no more on it," Mrs. Wainwright said.

With her narrow, sterile, stoical lips she looked from Con to Bella, then to Matty and again to Con. Finally she fixed her bright sparrow-eyed gaze on Matty and said:

"You were hours a-new measuring for a pair of shoes anyway, weren't you?"

He did not answer.

"You know what size she takes. You mended the other pair."

Bella sat quiet between them, staring, not speaking. Some minutes later she looked up and caught on the face of Mrs. Wainwright a curious expression of tight-lipped condolence that might have been half directed at the face of Con. It was very hard sometimes to tell what the brain behind the grim, pursed little face of Mrs. Wainwright was thinking. Her lips were sometimes a shield for an expression of delicate and far-off bemusement in the eyes.

"You might be thinking it was me," the girl thought. "It was my fault — That's what you might be thinking."

In this way, under the first hint of conflict, she felt herself pushed forward into a new phase with the Wainwrights — but how far and what kind of phase she did not know until, three weeks later, Jedd came home.

V

IT was Jedd, coming home on furlough at the end of July, with a corporal's stripes on his sleeves, a few days before the first brown-horned fields of wheat were ready for reaping on the strong clay lands above the town, who made her laugh once more. It was he, enormous, spirited and jovial, not at all unlike a droll big-toothed horse, who finally woke her.

From the first Wainwright behaved towards him as to a prodigal, riotously returned. They were less like father and son together than two boys of an age, roaring at play.

"Sergeant!"

"Corporal?"

"Are we all present and correct, sergeant?"

"Right on the nail, corporal. One — two — three — four — five — six — and Miss Ford, seven. Yes, corporal, all present and correct!"

"Then if we're all present and correct, sergeant, *what do we say?*"

"*Let 'em all come,* corporal! — one and all, *let 'em all come,* that's what we say!" As the stentorian roars shook the little kitchen Mrs. Wainwright would say:

"Folks'll hear you in the next county. And you — " she would tighten and shake at Wainwright a pair of lips that seemed to have no humor in them at all except the smallest dancing bird-prints at the edges — "You're wuss'n he is, you grut clown! I ought to fetch the copper stick to the pair on you — you grut daft jabeys, you!"

"Mother, you seem to forget we now have a corporal in the house."

"Anybody might think we had a regiment of artillery, you make noise a-new."

"And Miss Ford, how is Miss Ford?" At once, with light mockery, in jovial demonstrations of public affection, Jedd had begun to call her Miss Ford. "Keeping fair to mid, Miss Ford? Very fair, seemin'ly, and much mid, I think. I like Miss Ford's mid, sergeant, don't you? Miss Ford has filled out since we saw her last — there's a little more plush on the upholstery."

"Oh! Jedd, what a case you are."

She had not seen him since the night she had first arrived in the house. Her recollection of his face had always remained slightly twisted and vague, a little out of focus. Now he seemed to her almost too clear and muscular a reality. Something in the bantering soldier's way of talking gave him a curious physical familiarity, an impact sharper than that of either Con or Matty, so that she seemed to have known him for years. "Jedd, you fool. What a case you are." She felt the blood pricking and dancing in her throat. For the first time there were tears of laughter in her eyes.

"And how's the wheat looking, sergeant?" — Jedd pronounced it with long broad midland vowels — "wheeart — and th' ooarts, sergeant, how are th' ooarts?"

"Oncommon well, corporal. Wheeart's very near as tall as you are."

"And wheerabouts do we slap into it this year? Forty Acre? Or Wyman's piece?"

"Wyman's — and I count you never seen a field like it. It stands up like a regiment o' steel-backs. It'll be like rippin' through a field o' bamboo."

"Any on it laid?"

"Not a straw, corporal. And won't be if we live and have good luck till Monday."

"We'll slap it down in no time," Jedd said, — "you a-rippin', and me a-rippin', and Con a-rippin' and Matty like the cow's tail, rippin' on behind. And Miss Ford — don't forgit we got Miss Ford. She'll be a-mekking bonds faster'n we can rip. Bella — did you ever mek a bond?"

"I don't think so, Jedd."

"Then it's time I give y' a lesson. Come on — come along o' me now and walk as far as Wyman's and I'll show y' how to mek a bond."

"She's got summat else to do," Mrs. Wainwright said, " 'ithout traipsing out to Wyman's just to mek a bond."

"Summat else?"

"Yes, and summat better, a' shouldn't wonder."

"Better? Summat better? Summat better'n walking as far as Wyman's with Corporal Wainwright? — Why, my gal, there's nothing better'n that from here to Barrackpoore! — Come on, Bella, git your lid on. We're goin' to mek a bond."

"And you needn't keep her up there with your fool talk half the afternoon," Mrs. Wainwright said, "so there. You jes' git back here by four o'clock. I s'll mash the tea then whether you're back or not — and you needn't horse-face at me if it's cold."

"Be back in two cracks of Colonel Bum-Bum's whip," Jedd said. "It's Saturday. The sergeant and me are goin' to stretch we legs as far as the market hill afore supper-time."

"Yes, and you can jes' be careful what you do up *there!*" she said.

As Bella walked across the fields with Jedd for the first time that Saturday afternoon she remembered going across the same footpath, on an evening of pale summer lightning and gentle hissing rain, with Con. In three weeks, on the strong land, the thick horned wheat had grown and browned and curled. There was a touch of warm black-brown on the tips of the great square ears that was like the feathers of a sparrow. Sunshades of pink convolvulus winked at the edges of the wall of wheat where they crept and twined in sun. Withered leaves of thistle were half-silver, half-rusty. Cracks in the clay were wide enough to swallow some of the big brown pebbles that lay everywhere under the ripe cane-yellow straw.

"You must watch your feet," he said. "You git your ankle in one o' them and you'll be like the old sergeant. Drop and carry one for the rest of your days."

She loved the broad, quick, careless way of talking, the drollness that was in neither Con nor Matty. The lips were fuller and more generous than Con's; there was a fleshiness, a softer, smoother rosiness in the under lip that reminded her of the young Ben Wainwright, handsome and flaunting in the pictures of shoemakers' outings.

"You git holt o' the straws like this. See?" He had cut with a jackknife a couple of dozen straws from the edge of the field. Now he divided them and dressed them level and straight with a long sweeping pull of his hands. "Then over and twist and lock — see? — and that's your bond."

The first flick and lock of the straws was like sleight of hand, too swift for her to follow.

"You didn't twig it?" he said, "did you? Too quick for you — look, I'll do it slower."

He untwisted the straws, brushed them out and crossed them again, just below the ears. His thumbs were enormous. They were broad and flattened as they held the straws together. She could smell the clean fresh scent of new-cut straw and she heard the beards of the wheat-ears rustling rough and silky as he twisted and locked them for the second time.

"Then you never twigged it, did you?" he said. He laughed. "I was jes' the same. I remember Dad showing me — I never did git it, the first twenty or thirty times. He was a bit quicker tempered them days and he give me a ding across the ear after about the two-dozenth time — God A'mighty, I could hear the angels singing hymns."

[84]

He untwisted the straws. Then he stood behind her and then reached over her shoulders and put the straws in her hands.

"Go on. Hold them. It's as easy as swallowin' pibbles. Over, twist and lock — and then pull tight on the lock at the end."

Her bond fell to pieces when she pulled it. He laughed and showed her the trick of it again, and then again, perhaps ten or a dozen times. "You must think I'm a poor fool," she said once and he said: "It's like skating. There's a knack in it. You git it all at once," and again she felt as if she were learning to walk, like a child, in a series of clumsy steps, stupid and faltering and groping like a fool.

Then: "You got it!" he said. "You got it. That's it. Pull! — it's locked!"

She pulled at the straw ends. Miraculously the bond was locked by the ears.

"How did I do it? I can't think now — " In wonder at herself she was laughing too. "I did it and now I can't remember — "

"You don't have to remember. It's as easy as shelling peas — you'll do it in your sleep now."

"I did it," she said. Softly she marveled at herself. Once more she could feel the blood, excited by laughter, tingling in her throat. "I felt such a fool — I never thought I would."

On the way home he threshed an ear or two of wheat in his hands. He stopped once and cupped his hands and blew out the chaff in dancing husks through the vent formed by his thumbs.

In his palms the grains lay dark gold, clean and ripe and brilliant, like so many ants' eggs, and he said:

"That's the color I want to see your face. I never liked the color you were. You were a terrible color, that night — "

"They said you sat up with me."

"A time or two."

"Nell said I used to scream out."

"Not while I was there. You never done nothing while I was there. You just — "

"Well, I'm all right now," she said. "I'm better now. I'm more myself now — "

"Not till we git that face another color," he said. "You git some color on that face. Then you can talk."

It was not possible to express what she felt about this and she could only smile.

"Harvest'll put it on, though," he said. "You git making bonds for a month and you won't know who you are."

As he said this they reached the stile at the end of the wheatfield. It was the stile over which Con had, with stiff, buttonholed Sunday courtesy, helped her a score of times that summer.

Now when they reached the stile Jedd had none of Con's intense stiff courtesy. He simply laughed and lifted her up by the waist and in a single high swinging movement put her down on the other side of the stile. She felt her long skirt swing outwards and a rush of air swim up through the funnel of it, blowing softly on her legs. A pin-point of excitement darted up through the center of her body as she sailed down to earth, making her give a little scream.

"Oh! Jedd, you startled me." Her eyes were shining. "You took me unawares. I wasn't ready for that."

Careless, slightly swaggering, wetting his lips with his tongue, he sat on the stile, grinning.

"You're as light as a sack o' goose feathers. I could throw you over a haystack."

"Opportunity's a fine thing."

"Your eyes are black." He was bending down, watching her. He was laughing, pressing his tongue against the white edges of his teeth. "You got the blackest eyes I ever seen."

"You tell all the girls that," she said. "All the girls in Salisbury, everywhere — "

"Did Con ever kiss you?" he said.

"No."

"What about Matty?"

"No."

He laughed softly, wetting his lips.

"What about me?"

"No."

"Ah! Come on, Bella," he said.

"What here?" She mocked him slightly. He darted out

[87]

with both hands and caught her lightly by the shoulders. "In broad daylight? — in the middle of the afternoon? — "

"It tastes the same," he said, "dark or daylight."

"No!" she said.

"The gates are locked," he said.

By closing his knees suddenly he had caught her body by the hips. "There'll be people coming," she began to say but he laughed again and presently her entire body was folded against him.

He kissed her and she did not protest. His lips were thick and soft but when he took them away again she felt her own were cool. He laughed down at her again and said:

"Well, how was that? Nice — it was nice, wasn't it?"

"You look as if you thought so."

"Bella," he said. He was holding her by the hands now. He was calmer, much quieter, not smiling. "Come out with me tonight. Come out with me — let's go somewhere."

"I couldn't."

"Ah! Why not? Why not?"

"I couldn't. I promised Con."

"Ah! Con?" he said. "Who's Con?"

"Con's been very nice to me," she said. "Everybody's been very nice." She felt touched by the thought of the three brothers into a rush of happiness. "You don't know how nice you've all been to me." She could feel the prick of tears in her eyes. "All of you. One way and another."

"That's what we're here for," he said. He seemed suddenly to be aware of the start of tears in her eyes. It seemed to strike him that perhaps he had been responsible for making them. Jovially he said: "The gates are unlocked." Then as he leaped down from the stile he brushed his lips with casual delicacy against the side of her face and said:

"Well, sometime, eh? Before I go back. I'll hire a trap from Joe Draper's and drive you out somewhere."

"With the gray horse?"

"With the gray horse." He was laughing again. She felt herself laughing too. Then as he lifted her by the waist, with one hand, and swung her down from the high verge to the road, he said: "One Sunday afternoon. We'll drive as long as you like. Anywhere — till bull's noon."

That night Wainwright and Jedd, with Nell and Mrs. Wainwright, walked up into the market square, Wainwright with peacock-pride in tight gray herring-bone tweed and a hard square hat, Jedd in scarlet jacket, cord breeches and spurs and the broad fresh corporal's stripes on his sleeves. His mustache had a pale golden brilliance, fierily glinting, at the waxen pointed edges. Mrs. Wainwright wore a high black hat with flowers of purple and gray on the brim. Nell had a gray costume and a pink-gray hat with what Mrs. Wainwright called "a fall."

In his buttonhole Wainwright had a clove-red carnation with a sprig of maidenhair. He carried his best walking stick, a heavy Malacca with a finishing band of silver which he waved with friendly gay-dog nonchalance every twenty yards or so, at acquaintances.

"Evening, master. How do, master," he said. "Rare day. All appearance on it for tomorrow."

"You needn't whittle for fear folks won't see you," Mrs. Wainwright said. "They'll see you time a-new 'ithout you shouting. They know Jedd's home."

"They don't know he's a corporal, though," Wainwright said with pride. "They don't know he ain't a plain trooper any longer."

"I don't see what difference that makes," she said with tartness. "He's Jedd just the same."

At half-past ten Nell came upstairs to where, in the small front bedroom, Bella lay awake, watching the green gaslight cross made by the street lamp on the low ceiling above the bed.

"Still awake?" Nell said, and Bella said, "Yes: awake. Just lying here."

"I didn't want to wake you," Nell said. The room was full of the rustle of tissue paper as she folded and packed away hat and veil and dress. "We left the two men talking. Like two women. You couldn't get a word in edgeways. We left them to it in the market square."

When the final rustle of tissue paper had died Nell got into bed and said, "Good night. I wouldn't wonder if they weren't still jawing there at chapel time," and Bella said, "Good night, Nell," and then lay for some time longer staring up at the light, not tired.

She did not know how long it was before she was

waked by the sound of crashing glass, a bottle thrown across the street below, and then a yell of voices. The street lamp was still alight. A woman's voice in a high shrieking laugh broke to a cackle, and then she heard Wainwright's voice laughing too, shouting:

"Queenie! Queenie, my old beauty! Here! Let's get holt on you. Oscar and Jedd are going to give you a ride. Corporal! — *what do we say?*"

She got out of bed and went to the window and looked out. Queenie Foster was sitting in the gutter, under the lamplight, and Wainwright was trying to lift her up. A man named Oscar Sanders was twined about the lamppost, yelling, "Where's my old partner? Where's Jedd?" and from beyond the ring of gaslight Jedd came rearing like a swaying cavalry horse. She heard the clash of spurs and the two of them began to lift Queenie Foster up. Then as they lifted her Wainwright shouted: "Corporal!" and Jedd let go of Queenie Foster and staggered to attention and saluted and roared:

"Sergeant!"

"Is the whole troop present and correct, corporal?"

"All present and bloody near correct, sergeant!" Jedd said. "As bloody near correct as they ever will be!"

"Then if we're all present and correct, corporal, *what the Hanover do we say?*"

And then all four of them together, the three men yelling, the woman shrieking:

"*Let 'em all come!* One and all — all together — *let 'em all come!*"

Then Wainwright slipped in the gutter and fell down and sat there with Queenie Foster, giggling. Jedd began to try to raise her up again, lifting her body and letting it fall and then lifting it, working it like a bellows. Then Oscar Sanders started to climb the lamppost, singing:

> *When I was in the Queen's Hussars,*
> *A young rip-roaring touser,*
> *I met a female in a pub —*
> *And oh! she was a rouser!*

Before the end of this Oscar Sanders fell down. Most of the time Jedd charged up and down the pavement, in and out of the lamplight, shouting orders:

"Troop will move off at right diagonal! Sergeant!"

"Corporal!"

"Anybody seen Colonel Bum-Bum?"

"Left him in the bar!" Oscar Sanders roared. "Old Colonel Bum-Bum — got left in the bunghole!"

"Some say good old Bum-Bum!" Jedd yelled, "but what do we say?"

And all together again, Queenie Foster shrieking:

"We say —— Colonel Bum-Bum! That's what we say!"

Bella stood at the window for some time longer, watching, laughing to herself. When she went back to bed at last the four of them in the street below were locked together in a tangled string that wound up and down the street, yelling another song.

"*Rolling round the town!*" she heard them singing. "*Knocking people down! — having a rare old booze a-bet*

— tasting every kinda wet," and it was the sound of singing that woke Nell, who turned sleepily in the light of
the street lamp and said:

"Who is it? Whatever is it? It must be Ponto Simpson
or Cracky Robinson or somebody from the end of the
row."

"Go to sleep," she said. "It's just a few of them going
home."

"What are you laughing at?"

"It's Jedd and your father and Oscar Sanders and
Queenie Foster."

"Oh! No." Nell was sitting up in bed, folding and un-
folding her hands. "He's never broke out for years. He's
never done it for years. Now he'll be on a blinder for
weeks and weeks — "

"Lie down and go to sleep again," Bella said. "They'll
just have fat heads in the morning. That'll teach
them — "

"You've never seen him on a blinder. He'll be on it
for weeks — day in, day out, all through harvest."

"He's just happy for Jedd."

"It's not that," Nell said. "It's the beginning of a
blinder."

Long after the last yell from the street outside Bella
lay watching the ceiling, thinking of Jedd. She remembered how he had taught her to make a bond. She remembered how difficult it had been and how at last, before she knew how, it had come to be suddenly easy, like
a trick. She thought of the way he had trapped her by

[93]

the arms and hips, with his knees, and said to her, "The door's locked," and how he had wanted her face to have the color of the wheat grains and how finally he had kissed her and she had not protested.

"Now what?" she thought. She lay thinking of Con and Matty. She remembered the jealous formal tenderness of one and the expressive moving way the other had of using his hands. "Now what?" she thought. After she had thought of them each in turn she thought of Jedd alone, apart from the others. "Perhaps I'm closer to Jedd. He was the one who sat with me. I'm closer to Jedd. I must be. That was why I wanted him to kiss me."

The street lamp did not go out all night. In its light she did not sleep well. In the morning, waking late, she heard the sound of horse hoofs in the street outside and then of wheels crunching and a crowd of voices.

From the window she looked down on Wainwright, half dressed, and Mrs. Wainwright, wearing a grim little cloth cap with a long black glass hatpin in it. The pin seemed to go through the hat and then through the stern pursed face of Mrs. Wainwright and finally through Wainwright himself to pin him against the low fence beyond.

"Look at her," she was saying. "Take and have a good look at her. Look at her afore they take her way. For I'm burned if they won't take you one day — that's where you'll end. That's where they'll take you."

In terrible silence Wainwright stood crucified by the hatpin. The sound of cab wheels turning and of horse hoofs clattering on the Sunday morning air did not stir him. The cab with its drawn blinds hiding Queenie Foster clattered past Number Sixteen like the final coach of a funeral that had lost its hearse.

"As if they wasn't trouble a-new!" Mrs. Wainwright said. "As if we don't have to slave enough for the little bit we get."

A day later harvest began.

VI

AUGUST began with mornings of thin soft cloud that cleared before noon into days that shimmered with heat, in silence, under blue-white skies. From the cottoned valley the white mist of summer drew off rapidly, leaving a river low and sluggish in scorched meadows, bright as opaque glass. All along the white central valley, so far from the sea, heat locked itself in, burning windlessly on cracked clay lands, over brown-burnt beanfields and on acres of blistered wheat and whiter barley.

The men struck into the wheatfields every morning by five o'clock. As the heat of morning rose they put pebbles into their mouths and sucked them against the thirst of the day. They worked in a diagonal line, Wainwright leading, then Con and Jedd, with Matty behind. After them, sharper than ever, hungrily concentrated, lips nipped in, Mrs. Wainwright raked the rows of fallen wheat into sheaves that Nell and Bella tied.

At first Bella was not quick enough. She had not worked for seven or eight months and her hands were soft and sensitive. The scythed ends of the thick wheat stalks were like sharpened quill pens; they stabbed her as she bonded them and soon her arms were raw. It took her some time too to master the trick of tying the sheaf with its bond. Her hands did not seem big enough or strong enough to hold the bunched ears firmly while she locked the tail-straw under. So, at first, her sheaves were sloppy. The loose bonds broke as they were lifted.

Every now and then, for the first two or three days, the men would be coming back to help her.

"Can't you match it, Bella? Look, I'll show you. Get your knee on it. You must get your hand down tight, like this, see? — and then round and under."

"It looks simple. I'm buck-fisted, that's all — "

"You got to be quick," they told her, "and get it tight and nip it under."

Then one or other of them would bustle along the rows of untied sheaves and sweep out bond after bond, swiftly, tying them in a flash, so that in a few minutes her row was finished and she was level again with Nell. And sometimes Jedd, sweat streaming down his face and arms and chest. would find time to tease her for a moment. He would call her Miss Ford and set her laughing; so that Mrs. Wainwright would call, in a voice dry and biting:

"Ain't we got work a-new 'ithout you two a-foolin' like a pair o' wet 'uns?"

Sometimes Con would skim the whetstone savagely down the scythe edge as if he were crossing swords. "The army must be gittin' loony these days."

"The army's all right. It's some o' the folks outside it."

"Ah?"

"Ah! an' I'll laugh with who I want and when I want."

"Ah! an' you'll very like laugh th' other side o' your face these days."

"Any road, it's a nice bright day." Always Jedd, as Wainwright was so proud to say, would remain the great droll, imperturbable and unheated, giving the last soft answer. "Long as the milk don't turn."

Then, stony and dry and biting again, the voice of Mrs. Wainwright would cut the two of them finally apart:

"More sense if you'd git on with what you should do instead o' gripin' and grizzling and horse-facin' at one another so much. You urge anybody to death, moanin' and horse-facin' all day long."

"I laughed," Jedd would say. "Is they summat wrong wi' laughing?"

It was always Mrs. Wainwright, tart and tireless, spirited as a weasel, who would not let them rest. It was always she, at noon, when the seven of them lay in the shade of an elm, pillowed on sheaves, grasping at a few moments of coolness, drying their sweat, who got first to her feet and whipped the men back into the high heat of afternoon.

"Layin' here like a lot o' pigs on straw — I'll be burned if some on you wouldn't lay here till bull's noon if anybody'd let you."

And once she even turned on Bella, sitting on a sheaf some way behind the rest, in the hot choking afternoon, with her head between her hands:

"I'd bring my bed with me tomorrow if I were you, my lady."

"My head went round, that's all."

"Very like it wouldn't go round quite so much if folks wasn't always tryin' to turn it."

It was continually as if, in the back of her mind, a dark canker of dread was working, gnawing and fretting and driving her on: the dread that winter might be hard or long or workless or even, if they did not scrape enough from harvest, without bread. Bitten hard into her mind were the days of barley-pap, the gray years of bread and scrat, the iron of weeks when Wainwright was out on a blinder, fighting lampposts. "If we live and have good luck," was the warning she brought to every hint or thought or plan for the future. "Don't you dare burn bread," was her deadly and terrible threat to those who wasted, "you'll come to want, sure as God's above, you'll come to want" — a flaming sign of evil more stunning and more fearful than all the dry long reams of Wainwright's wandering Wesleyan prayer.

Her sons were the arteries of her living. She did not want them ever to be cut away from her; she wanted to be there with them always, urgently driving, tirelessly pumping the blood of her own dread and spirit into them so that the scarecrow of want could be kept away. She remembered the days when she had no hands to help her in the harvest field, raking and bonding and even scything side by side with Wainwright, the children coming too fast, one quick after another, three dying, so that

sometimes she had two of them at the breast together —
"one a-nussin' and one a-stannin' — both on 'em at what
skinny drop o' milk I got, and a mite that was, I tell
you."

She had driven them from the first, jealous for them
and deep-bitten with the dread of which she never spoke;
so that even now she looked on them as children who
were recalcitrant, quarreling, not to be trusted when her
back was turned. "I got to be roundin' up on 'em all the
time. Ben never will. I got to keep 'em at it. Ben talks a
lot, but that's as far as it ever gits with him."

So in the harvest field she was, if anything, more watch-
ful of them than she ever was in the house or the shop
or the street at home. The winter's bread was there; the
weather was right for harvest; there was no time for
fooling now. She knew that Jedd had always fooled; Jedd
had always been the fooling, the unruffled, the casual-
hearted one. It was true, as Wainwright said, that Jedd
could never be put out. She never forgot that it was Con
who could be roused so quickly. It was Con, as she said,
that you couldn't turn.

But that summer she saw that it was different; it was
not quite the same now, with a girl in the field. If spring
and early summer had never troubled her in that way it
was simply because she hardly ever thought of Bella as
a girl. The thin, vague, flat-chested husk that a man could
lift with one hand had hardly seemed much more than a
ghost of a backward child.

But now, after a few days, she saw that there was more

in her than a mere change of mind and body. It was not simply that her skin, naturally dark, was browning quickly, level and smooth under the harvest sun; or that she was filling out more rapidly, eating ravenously, her blood brightening and her breasts round and nimble again; or that she laughed more. It was much more as if all that the three brothers had done for her, Con with sober devotion, Matty with delicate hands and at last Jedd with a soldier's foolery and a soldier's laughter, had succeeded in coaxing her back to flower together. Between them they had helped to bring her forward to a moment when, like a bud, she was ready to break open. The sun had done the rest.

And Mrs. Wainwright, as she watched and goaded and urged her sons, watched this too. She watched the quick turn of the dark head, the hair pretty and sun-touched, as it lifted from a sheaf. She saw her way of laughing with her tongue slightly out, pink and fresh against open lips. She even saw Wainwright, cowed and uneasy in a new phase of conversion, caught in an occasional mild act of admiration, surprised out of himself by some supple turn of the brown figure as it moved in the sun.

"She's got eyes a-new glued on her 'ithout you making any," she said. "You'll be mowin' your own legs off one o' these days if you don't look at what you should do."

Then it was her birthday. She had, at first, three presents for her birthday. It was some time later before the fourth one came from Con. The shoes made by Matty had been finished for some time: he had stayed on in the shop, alone, to make them in the evenings. They were neat plain shoes of calf with buckles, and the buckles were in the shape of a bird that looked like a swallow, flying enclosed in a silver ring. He had spent the whole of a Saturday afternoon and evening in the shops of Bedford, choosing the buckles, and when the shoes were given her at last Wainwright took them with tender appraisal out of her hands.

"They're a good shoe, they are. You won't see a better shoe nowhere n' that. He's a craft, Matty is. He's a rare craft, that boy."

She was touched by the gift of the shoes. They lay in a box on the kitchen table, casually, on the Sunday morning of her birthday. There was no sign of Matty and Mrs. Wainwright said, tersely:

"I don't know what 'tis, so it ain't a bit o' use you askin' me. He just left it there and said that's for Bella and skived off out somewhere."

Too shy to give her the shoes himself, he was still shyer as he listened later to her thanks for them.

"I don't know about the buckles," he said. "If you don't like the buckles I can get 'em changed. They said I could change them."

"The buckles are beautiful," she said.

"They cost more'n a bread check, I warrant," Mrs. Wainwright said.

"Not all that much."

"No?" she said. "I knowed times a-new when I could ha' done with the few ha'pence you had back out of half a sovereign. Well, they ought to do somebody a good turn of a Sunday — for I'm burned if they ain't a sight too good for weekdays. I never had such shoes."

From Nell there was a neckband: black, of three-quarter-inch velvet, clasped at the back with a simple pair of hooks. The pier glass above the fireplace in the kitchen was hung rather high for the benefit of the three tall sons and Wainwright, who struggled in front of it with starched dickies and three-inch collars, beeswaxed to the gloss of ivory, on Saturdays and Sundays. But it was too high for both Nell and Bella, who used the fireside stool to stand on so that they could see themselves.

"They're all the go now," Nell said. The black band of velvet had something of the same aristocratic uplifting effect on Bella as the jet necklace Arch Wilson had given her. "All you want now is earrings —"

"Who says so?" Mrs. Wainwright said.

"Bella's dark," Nell said. "She'd look nice with earrings. They'd suit her."

"And who's got money to throw away on earrings? Nobody as *you* know, my gal."

"I wish they had."

"Wish! — wish!" Mrs. Wainwright said.

"Who's horse-facin' this time?" Jedd said, and a second later picked up Bella by the tips of her elbows, so that she could see in the glass.

"Put the gal down," Mrs. Wainwright said, "foolin' here while I got my hands full —"

"It's her birthday," Jedd said. "And I'll tell you what.

Me and her are trottin' out this afternoon. I got the trap from Joe Draper's. And if you don't believe me, look outside."

"I wonder you didn't get a landau," Mrs. Wainwright snapped, "and a coachman to drive!"

Tethered to the street lamp was a high black trap with copper side lamps, black-and-white check seats, and a gray horse, and in it, that afternoon, halfway through harvest, he drove her out, eastward, to country she had not seen before. The thin spires of the valley gave way to stouter, stockier churches of stone surrounded by villages of thatch, with walls of pale ochre and white and light sienna and chalky rose. Farms were held in hollows broken by cool spinneys of oak. Fields of wheat and barley, half cut, were small and sheltered and fringed with dykes of pink-gray willow herb. The open feeling of the wide windy valley, of Nenweald perched in smoky exposure on the edge of it, between its background of strong clay and its green apron of stronger meadowland, was lost in a long afternoon of sun sultrily caught and held between the unvarying gentle hollows, the little colored villages and the spinneys of dark shade. There was hardly a sound except always, monotonously, the little song of yellow-hammers beating and deepening the silence of the hot air and from far off, behind brows of woodland, the surprised rare chime of bells.

Towards late afternoon Jedd said, "If the sergeant was here I should be thinking it was time for a wet. I'm that hungry too — hungry as a thacker," and presently they stopped at one of the small thatched ochre-walled pubs for a plate of bread and cheese and a glass of beer.

She was wearing the velvet band round her neck and the shoes that Matty had made for her. As she got down from the trap he noticed that already the white dust of the hot narrow roads had covered the shoes with the slightest bloom. He took out his handkerchief and she put first one foot and then the other on the iron step of the trap so that he could dust the shoes.

"You know what I'm going to do before I go back?" he said. "I'm going to take you over to Evensford and get your photo taken. They got a new place there now."

"I had it taken once," she said.

"I want one how you look now," he said. "Just like that."

There was one more moment, that day, which she afterwards remembered with happiness. On the way back they tethered the horse for half an hour on the verge of the road. The country was a little higher there and down below them she could see, shiplike on a sea of grass, between islands of cedar and elm and purple copper beech, the south front of a big house, with a long stone terrace and rows of red-striped awnings down at the windows against the sun.

"I couldn't be any happier if I lived in a great house like that," she said. "I wouldn't want to be any happier. I know I couldn't be."

After some time she lay down on the grass and put her hands under her head and looked up at the sky. The beer had made her drowsy. The aftertaste of it made her re-member days at the Three Bells, when she could have half a pint of ale with her bread and cheese at eleven o'clock and another half pint, if she wanted it, at half-past five. She ran her tongue over her lips and shut her eyes. She had been very happy in those days before Arch Wilson came: young and eager and excited, perhaps too excited when wagonettes of fishermen came in summer and the flat lands were breezy with dry east winds and the bar parlor loud with men drinking and flattering and calling her names. Things had gone wrong a bit after that, but that day she was sure, as she lay there in the ripe seed-dusty grasses and the last rose titty-bottles of clover and the gray-mauve scent-bottle of plantain flower, that the wrongness and trouble of them was fully and finally over.

Jedd roused her with brushings of grass-seed across her lips. She opened her eyes. She laughed and tried to seize the grass in her teeth. Jedd laughed too and drew the stalk away, so that she lifted her head and bit at it sev-eral times until she was tired of biting.

"Oh! you and your grass," she said.

Suddenly he was lying beside her, turning her face to him, kissing her. She let herself be kissed for some time before she opened her eyes and looked beyond him at the high blue sky. She realized then that the effect of the kiss was something like the pleasant air of the afternoon. It simply warmed her with tender drowsiness. It was part of the mild, summery, unexacting air.

"I'll miss you like Hanover," Jedd said.

"You'll have my photograph."

"This time I'll write to you," he said. "Could you write to me?"

"Yes," she said. "I'll write to you."

There was one more incident that afternoon. At the foot of the hill an acre or so of marsh, by the side of a little stream, was covered with osiers that were already burnt ripe, a smooth pale orange, by August sun. A small two-storied house with a thatched roof stood half hidden in the middle of the osier beds, at the end of a built-up path.

"Blamed if I didn't think so." Jedd pulled up the trap and looked at the house. "This is where Dad and me used to come to get a new clothes basket or a dinner basket. A man named Sherwood used to live here. Dad said they were the best baskets you could get. He used to let us gather water cress. Best water cress you ever tasted. He said there was iron in the stream."

He stood up in the trap and looked over the hedge, across the osiers. The door of the house was closed. Two windows were shuttered.

"There was just him and his missus. It's been a minute ago too — when I was a kid," Jedd said. "Probably died. They used to do teas, I recollect, at one time."

"There's nobody there," she said.

"If there was," he said, "nobody would ever think of looking."

"What do you call this place?" she said.

"I fancy they call it Slapton Springs."

He let the horse walk for most of the rest of the way home. There was no sense, he said, in rushing back with something he'd paid for. Presently it became time for the lamps to be lighted. In the smoky golden glow of the candles he drove with one hand, holding her waist with the other.

"You wouldn't marry me," he said, "would you?"

That was exactly the way, she thought, she would have expected him to ask her. She stared for a few moments at the gray smooth flanks of the horse before she answered.

"Not this time," she said. The words were almost the same she had used to Con. "Not now — "

"Which time then?" he said. "Next time?"

"Ask me next time."

She turned and kissed his face. It was impossible to tell him, in that moment, what she felt about him and how happy she was. She was beginning to be aware, without being able to express it, that there were many sorts of happiness. She put her hand on his shoulder. She touched the band of velvet on her throat and looked up at the night hung with black tenderness beyond the carriage lamps. Bright harvest stars went swinging across the valley and she was almost afraid, in the pure suspense of it, to speak again. "Because," she thought, "it's like a spell or something. It's so quiet. It might never happen again and I don't want to break it."

"I'd die for you," Jedd said and looked suddenly so

roused and military and flustered that she laughed and said:

"Oh! goodness, I hope not. I hope nobody'll ever have to do that for me."

He laughed, droll as ever. "I'd die laughing anyway."

After that there was, for a time, no present from Con. Long afterwards she said to Matty: "Perhaps if I'd never had a birthday that year things would never have happened like they did. It was my birthday that began it — you with the shoes and Nell with the neckband and Nell saying I ought to have earrings and Jedd driving me out that day. That was what began it. If it hadn't been for that perhaps there wouldn't have been that day in the harvest field. And then that other day."

It was three days after Jedd had driven her out with the gray horse and trap that he suddenly turned to her in the harvest field, at the end of dinner hour, and saw that she was sleepy. She was sitting with her back to the trunk of an oak and her eyes began swimming as she nodded her head.

He had been full of banter all through the hot morning, calling her Miss Ford and sometimes, in light mockery, her ladyship. There were two days of his furlough to go. "Tonight, if her ladyship pleases, we must get the photo," he said. "Seven o'clock tonight. We got to have the photo." He worked always in trousers and a thick army singlet, his braces buttoned and looped down over his hips over the broad buckled belt that held his whet-stone.

He laughed softly as he saw her dozing against the trunk of the tree and said:

"Come on, my lady. If you want to have a nap you'd better nap comfortable. Come on — have a lay-down on a sheaf somewhere."

Con and Matty and Wainwright had already picked up their scythes and were walking away across the stubble, in the sun, when he stooped and lifted her in his arms.

She let out a little cry. She said something about losing herself for a moment and not knowing where she was and how Jedd had startled her. The small high sound of her voice, almost a shriek, made each of the men turn round.

"Put me down, Jedd. I'm not sleepy. I don't want to —"

"Ah! come on, have five minutes. You can't keep your eyes open. It'll do you good. Put your head on a sheaf somewhere."

"No — let me down now, Jedd, please."

"Her ladyship ought to rest. Then she'll be nice and fresh for the photo —"

"Put her down!"

Jedd turned in time to see Con rushing back across the stubble, swinging the scythe. He was running with the blade of the scythe held at the perpendicular, point downward, like the head of an axe. He was runing madly, yelling, "Put her down! Put her down! Can't you hear what she says, you blamed fool — put her down!"

Three or four yards away he made a violent downward swing with the blade. It struck the outer branches of the oak tree. A young branch was ripped down and with it a shower of leaves and acorns. As it fell he ripped at it again, crossways this time, at the horizontal, and Jedd actually felt the whip of the air as the blade of the scythe struck the oak bough and beat it away.

A moment later he dropped Bella out of his arms, throwing her behind him. He was still good-humored, still laughing, as Con came at him a second time with the scythe.

"Hold hard," he said. "Don't get over your collar. It's hot — "

"Shut up afore I pin you against the bloody tree!"

Con swung the scythe again. The point whipped wildly in a curve that was not more than ten or twelve inches from Jedd's chest. Nell screamed from across the stubble. Jedd took a step or two backwards, slipping on the roots of the tree. As he fell he saw the scythe coming at him for the third time, again at the perpendicular, point downwards, like an axe.

This time it actually came down, hitting a tree root, point stiff in the bark. Out of sheer habit he was still laughing, but now his voice was somewhere between a laugh and a yell, and Con was screaming hoarsely:

"I've had enough! I've had enough!" trying at the same time to wrench the scythe point from the bark.

Jedd scrambled backwards. He was still calm. He kept his eye clear and fixed as he reached back for the handle of Bella's wooden rake where she had left it propped by the trunk of the tree.

He levered himself to his feet with the handle. He held the rake in front of him, cool, still grinning. He set his feet wide apart. He could see the fair, red-shot, molten eyes of Con blind with sweat and he kept them fixed with his own.

"All right, my old beauty, come on now. Have a go. Pick where you like."

The blade came at him again: this time in a diagonal downward cut, aimed at the shoulder. He parried it with the wooden tines of the rake. The scythe edge stuck in the head of the rake as it had stuck in the root of the tree and Con fought to wrench it loose, yelling.

"You'll hurt somebody in a minute," Jedd said. "I s'll have to deal with you in a minute."

Con came at him again. He took several steps backwards, calm, watching, feeling his way outwards from underneath the tree. He saw Con slash at him again and this time slip, as he had done himself, on the exposed roots of the tree. He went half down on one knee, trying to save himself with the scythe.

It was the chance Jedd had waited for. He started running and threw the rake as he ran. It hit the scythe in the bow of the handle, partly knocking it from Con's hands and Con yelled:

"I'll get you! I'll get you. I'll kill you, you bastard!"

Jedd was running, calm, long-striding, across to the middle of the stubble, to where he had left his scythe. He looked back once, his eye in its cool trained way measuring the distance. He judged he had thirty or forty yards. He heard Nell crying loudly and his father bawling "Drop it, you blamed fools, drop it I tell you!" and then something from his mother in her thin wiry wrath about "if I git anyways near the pair on you!" and he was aware that she was running too.

He must have had fifteen seconds or so to kick the iron staple out of the head of his scythe, so that the blade came free. He was calm enough to pick up a pebble at the last moment of running and he gave the staple the third, final hit with that.

Then he was holding the blade in his right hand, like a sword. Then he had a sheaf in the other, his hand deep in the middle of it, like a shield.

Across the stubble, swerving and leaping among the flat sheaves, the scythe swinging and flashing in the sun, Con came running as if he did not see him. "Like a damn' dervish," Jedd thought. He stood with his feet wide apart again, waiting. His head was lowered, the sheaf covering the front of his body. Across the field, over towards the tree, his mother was shouting something to Bella and from out of the shadow of the tree Bella was throwing a rake.

"Come on, my beauty," he said. He wiped a drip of sweat from the lower half of his face with the back of his hand. "We're a waitin' — "

Then the scythe came down at him again, perpendicular, swinging down like an axe. He parried with the sheaf, meeting the blade full on the side step as he threw the sheaf. He aimed the sheaf so that the body of it hit the scythe and the mass of horns on the beards struck upward, into the face of Con.

The weight of the sheaf knocked the scythe to the ground. Con fell backwards over another sheaf behind him. Jedd ran with the scythe blade swinging wide like a sword, still grinning. Then he had Con pinned on the sheaf, his body like a seesaw across it, the head lowest, pressed against the stubble wires.

'Shall I slit your gizzard?" he said. "Shall I? like they do the damn' dervishes?" He still spoke of it as if it were the joke of a hothead. The face below was a mess of molten sweat. There was nothing cruel in its moist dark flush of rage and he did not hate it. "Ah! you buck-fisted mad-brain — you never did look where you were running, did you?"

A moment later he gave the sword a circular flourish above his head, cavalry-fashion, as if he really meant to bring it down.

"Zlick! — "

It was meant to be like the sound of a slitting throat. He laughed as he saw Con pull back his head, terrified at last, trying to draw it free.

"Look out! — I'll cut your blamed head off an' show it to you!"

A moment later his mother hit him a crushing blow on

the back with the rake. He dropped the scythe, more out of astonishment than pain, and fell on his knees. Then she hit Con with the rake, first on the legs, then on the hips and backside. Then, as Jedd knelt there, she hit him on the backside. She hit both of them ten or a dozen times on the backside. The blows were so quick that they could not get up between them and now and then she screeched:

"I'll warm your arses, the pair on you, big as you are. I'll warm your arses!"

Then Jedd was running and she was after him. He could not run very fast now because of laughing. She had a great advantage with the rake handle and sometimes she hit him a blow on the shoulders. Then he spurted between the sheaves and she could not catch him and she went back for Con.

"I'll gie you a taaste on it too!" she screeched.

Then he was running, weaving among the sheaves. She was too quick for him and presently she was hitting him on the shoulders, making him dance with pain.

"Ah! I'll make you dance!" she said. "I'll make you dance, you great jabey. I'll knock some sense into your big head even if I have to knock it through your arse!"

She gave him another welting blow that cracked on his bare elbows as he lifted them and from a distance Jedd taunted her:

"Hit somebody your own size, woman!" and then everybody, even Nell, was laughing.

Only Mrs. Wainwright stood grim in the sun, in the

center of the field, among the flat sheaves of wheat that looked as if she herself had flayed and flattened them, a little gray burning figure of wrath, defiant.

"Ah! you may laugh!" she said. "But I ain't laughin'. I'm cussed if I see anything to laugh at. That I tell you!"

Four teeth of the wooden rake were broken from the blows she had given them and Wainwright said:

"You better get a fresh rake, Bella. There's another one underneath the tree."

Alone, under the tree, in the coolness out of the sun, she stood for some moments watching the Wainwrights. They were already reaping and raking and bonding again among the corn. The laughter had finished now.

She stood thinking of the flash and flourish of the scythe blade as Jedd, whirling it cavalry-fashion, had brought it down above his brother's head. The swing of the blade, in its whipping curve, came terribly back to her.

"He could have murdered him," she thought.

After that the end of summer, merging into autumn, was quieter. Jedd went back from furlough, jocular, allowing no hint of sadness in farewell, never mentioning again the fact that she could not marry him, taking with him a picture of herself standing by a marble fern-stand under an operatic fern, with the velvet band round her neck and her dark hair piled high.

When Mrs. Wainwright saw the picture she appeared to ponder on it bleakly.

"H'm," she said. "You can see who 'tis."

By the middle of September the wagons had left the fields. Like pecking hens the gleaners invaded the stubbles. The gleaning bell no longer rang, as it had done in Mrs. Wainwright's childhood, morning and evening, as if for the start and finish of a hungry race, but the race was still there — "I'll be burned if some on 'em don't scrat to get there fust," Mrs. Wainwright said, "I wonder they don't bed out there" — and crowds of women and children and even shoemakers broke from the town at dawn and returned to it, trucks and barrows and even gocarts piled high with sacks, heads holding vast sheet-balloons of corn, at night. Mrs. Wainwright, Nell and Bella gleaned on to October. By that time the stubbles were striped green with the weeds of autumn and the meadows below were green once again with grass that was fresh and acid against the pale mist-blue sky. And when the last corn ear had been dropped to the Wainwrights' pile in Wyman's stackyard, where later the thresher would deal with it like a widow's mite at the end of the ten great Wyman ricks, Mrs. Wainwright could look at it with much the same bleakness as she had looked at Bella's picture and say:

"Well: it's nothing like we had that year Nell was a little mite. But we must be thankful for what we *have* got. We'll get through — if we live and have good luck."

Some time before this Bella was aware of a change of attitude in Con. Uneasily and hesitantly he began to hang about the kitchen, the yard and the ash path that cut the narrow garden in half. In exasperation Mrs.

Wainwright whipped him with her tongue — "Keep mor-tarin' in and out, in and out, for everlastin' trampin' through! Why the nation don't you sit down or git on out and make yourself scarce somewhere?"

The end of this was a rushing awkward maneuver by which, one October evening, he went through the front door of the house and trapped Bella as she came through the entry from the back.

"I got 'em a week or two back. Nell said that's what you wanted. I couldn't get them for your birthday — not the sort she said would suit you."

She stood staring at the earrings as she held them in the palm of her hand. Under the street lamp she could see that they were black, with small drops, like tears of jet. She did not know what to say to him in surprise or thanks or happiness and he said:

"They promised 'em that day in the harvest field, that Wednesday, when Jedd and me had a stack-up. But they didn't come. That's what made me mad. Are they the sort you wanted?"

"Yes," she said, "they're the sort I've always wanted."

But it was not the gift, the thought behind it or the material fact of it that touched and disturbed and im-pressed her. She was aware, first under the lamplight and then later, that same night, as she tried the earrings on in the kitchen, of a great change in himself. It was not only that he looked at her with a great awkward air of mascu-line embarrassment, as men so often do when they give presents to women, but that his eyes were shrouded, sad and engrossed with distances — the look of someone victimized.

It was too early even to make a guess, that night, at the depth of what he felt for her. She was simply aware of an imprisoned sadness, shorn of freedom, that could not express itself. She was conscious also, in herself, of a fascination that was confused. Beside him the natures of Jedd and Matty began to seem, now, remarkably innocent and unexacting. They were content to give and did not ask for much. But she was still unaware, that night, of how much, in time, he was to ask of her or of how much, in the end, he was prepared to give.

Presently, that autumn, she had another preoccupation.

"I ought to do something. Some work. It's time I earned my keep," she said.

"Work!"

The fatal and foreshadowed bitterness of Mrs. Wainwright's dread and goading flared up in the single word.

"Work! There ain't work a-new now for one shop, let alone twenty, and I'll lay there won't be that 'ithin a fortnit if things don't alter. Work! — You never bin here when there ain't no work, have you? I knowed the time when my chap never had a pair for thirteen weeks. That was lucky if you like, and me with Con and Jedd in ap'ons, hanging round me. Work — you can work all right, if there is any and we live and have good luck."

In this way the Wainwrights, with their sacks of grain threshed and stored in the coalhole under the stairs, prepared to face November. Farther up the valley, at Evensford, the last of the year's Feasts was over; there would be no other until July. Everybody, as Mrs. Wainwright remarked, might just as well shut the door and now, at last, claim winter.

VII

WINTER began with brusque wet storms from the west, that were followed by dry winds from the northeastward, the direction of the sea, and from which the valley had no protection. Over the bare easterly shoulder of land the wind had a way of skimming and pouring like invisible ice, pitching down to river level and then whipping up again to the westward hill, where the town lay raw and exposed, full in the lash of it.

By January the chimneys of the little back-yard shops were mostly smokeless; there was no longer a chorus of tapping. The noise of hand trucks running through dry streets on bare iron wheels was, except on Mondays, a skeleton echo. There was nothing, except on Mondays, to deaden the futile clatter of wheels racing to those factories that were open or part open in the hope that they might have a sleeve-full of uppers or even a single pair to offer. It was only on Mondays that the scurry of flat-capped women to pop shops gave to the truck wheels a deader, heavier sound.

By chance, every few days, Wainwright would hear of a hope of work in towns across the valley: a pair or two in Orlingford, a dozen at Nenborough, something at Evensford, a chance at Addington, nine miles away. "Git the truck out. Nip through Chapel Yard. Go down by Long Hedges so nobody don't twig you. And git back afore dinner if you can."

It was Nell who ran with the truck. She was a girl of deceptive plumpness, high in the cheekbones; with a puffy rosiness of bright flesh that had underneath it some touch of the bony yellow light of Mrs. Wainwright's skinny ivory. When she ran she was quickly out of breath. She had a way of running with her lips open, one hand holding a big pinned woolen scarf on her throat, her breath sobbing. In the cold air the colors of her face seemed gradually to intensify and then separate, draining away from each other until the puffy skin was all of Mrs. Wainwright's pallid shining ivory, except for tiny burns of bluish crimson fierce on the cheekbones.

Three doors from the Wainwrights lived a family named Mitchell, a man and a woman with a stunted epileptic son. Since the son could not run with the truck Mitchell ran with it himself: tall, undernourished, gangling down hills with the uncanny and sinister swiftness, half sideways, of a black-hatted crab. From behind steel-rimmed spectacles, tied round the back of his ears with a black bootlace, Mitchell had the crab's way of seeming always to look backwards, glinting with lidless eyes.

"Don't let Mitchy see you. Mitchy'll be off if he gits wind on it. Trust Mitchy to be on the mek-haste, trust Mitchy."

The rivalry of Mitchell, always mean, that winter seemed to become sharp and desperate. Mitchell became a sinister shadow recognizable at long distances by the thin-legged run and the peculiar high dome of the hard black hat. He still wore the long old-fashioned curve-tail coat, almost a frock coat, of twenty years before, and like the hat it had become green, as with a dust of mold, from years of fading.

He pushed, too, a truck that was unlike most others: a truck of basketwork, on two low back wheels and a third still lower one, at the front, like a caster. The truck was so balanced that Mitchell could sit on it at the back, paddling himself forward with one leg and then coasting with iron whistlings and clatterings down the hills.

It was this sound that pursued Nell as she gasped across and up the valley, desperate for work, that winter.

There were factories that began at six in the morning and sometimes she was out in darkness, running with bread in her hands. The lard on the thick coarse home-baked bread was as cold as snow on her teeth when she first began biting it. Then the bread itself, rammed down, seemed to become mixed with her sucked-in breath, congealing at the bottom of her throat into a cold clogging mass she could not swallow.

Then behind her, in the winter morning darkness, she would fancy that she heard the sound of Mitchell, coasting down the long valley hill on the truck. Sometimes it was Mitchell; sometimes the morning was bare of the sound of anyone but herself and her truck scouring through frozen pools. Mitchell or no Mitchell she was afraid of being late at the factories; there were always other runners. In the shabby little towns, in the windy morning darkness, the factories were lit mostly with mantleless gas flares, the flames fanwise, darkish yellow and blue-pricked if turned too high. But sometimes there were still oil lamps, nailed to whitewashed walls, with crinkled reflectors of tin in the shape of shells.

If the lock was still on a door she pulled the truck by the wall and waited. Troops of closing-girls came and waited too, black-pinafored, huddled against the yellow bricks of alleyways. It seemed that every factory was stuck in an alleyway, on a slope, down which the wind was narrowly driven, as into a funnel. Inside, too, the pattern and odor of them was the same; always the steep wooden stairs and the walls soaked with grease, always the dark imprisoned odor of leather, the sing and stink of gas flames, the hollow rattle of iron treadles on sewing machines.

And always Mitchell. She feared more than anything the moment of turning the corner of an alleyway and finding Mitchell's basket truck already there before her, pushed up against the wall. At the sight of the truck all the old stern dread of her mother, the grim terror of want, came rushing back to her and made her heart pound and curdle and grow sick.

One day as she climbed the stairs of a factory at Orlingford Mitchell came gangling down, crabwise, arms full of uppers. There is something about a boot upper, flapping, hollow, the tongue loose, the inner skin of lining gaping white, that is like a gutted fish. She felt a wave of nausea as Mitchell pounded past her. All her blood began to leap and drum into her face, thick and deafening, and a moment later she heard the voice of the forewoman as if through a screen:

"Only this minute give the last pair out. Won't be no more till the latter end of the week, if they is then."

As she stood at the head of the stairs she seemed to see them pitching down beyond their double flight into endless terrifying flights that were darkly swallowed in a pit. The figure of Mitchell seemed to be fumbling with the door. She felt ill with sickness and then the voice of the forewoman was calling:

"One o' my gals says Parsons's had a middlin' order in. She counts it was yesterday, else the day afore —"

"Parsons?"

"Over at Emberton. It's Will Parsons's brother, him at Orlingford. It's about halfway to Newport Pagnell — eight or nine mile. Might be ten."

As she turned to hurry down the stairs she saw Mitchell still at the foot of them, still in the pretense of fumbling with the latch. As he saw her turn he dragged the door open and scuttled out. She ran downstairs and out into the street and then heard, fifty yards away, the squeak and scrape of the basket truck as Mitchell paddled himself away.

She began running. It was nine miles to Emberton, nearer ten as the woman had told her, and for three hours

that morning she hurried, alternately walking and runing, under the illusion that Mitchell was somewhere in
front of her. Most of the road was new to her. She had an
idea that she had missed him in the streets about the factory. She ran as she always did, head forward, one hand
clutching her scarf, her mouth sucking air. That winter
there had been hardly any snow. Skies of a peculiar steely
grayness had given winds of great dryness that seemed
always to promise snow and then withhold it. Snow
seemed to become vaporized into piercing dusty air. As
she ran she heard this dry snowless wind crackling on
fields of cabbage leaves and through the black skeletons
of January woods and with a steady droning sing through
the cups of telegraph wires. Sometimes she saved a piece
of her bread to eat on her way back home, but that morning there had been nothing to save and she began to feel,
presently, as if the bones of herself were hollow. They
seemed fragile and terribly light, like the dead husks of
wild parsley stalks on the roadsides where she was running.

"Might be tuthri pair about dinnertime. Can you wait
till dinnertime?"

"Yes. Yes. I'll wait. I can wait."

"Where do you come from?"

"Nenweald."

"Things must be gittin' chronic."

She waited in the yard outside. There was always a sack
or two in the truck and now she wrapped them round
her shoulders. In the ear of one of them she could feel a

small round bump. She took the sack off her shoulders and put her hand in and found a small potato. She wrapped the sack round her shoulders again and ate the potato. She ate slowly, not so much cold as fragile and hollow with tiredness, vague and paralyzed.

Presently she realized that there was no Mitchell. The illusion that Mitchell had been always just in front of her had exhausted her more than all her running. She was wearily glad about Mitchell. At home they would be glad. The colors of her face, instead of separating into ivory and the two high burning sparks of bluish-rose, gradually became, as she sat there, only one color, the color of the inner flesh of the potato she had been eating. There had been in the potato the brownish mark of a worm, a dark crinkle she had scooped and bitten out, and now her eyes, the narrow hollow of her nostrils and the under-shadows of her cheeks began to have the same worm-gnawed, sickly air.

At two o'clock they found her half a dozen pairs. She was so cold that the joy she felt had no effect on her. Her jaws were so stiffened that she could not smile.

"We want 'em back pretty sharp," the checker said. "When can you git 'em back?"

"Oh! they'll sit up all night. They can sit up all night," she said.

"Things must be gettin' chronic, no mistake," the checker said.

She felt a certain unreal, dreamlike triumph as she went home out of one valley into another. The afternoon

was pierced by a wind which rose, at high exposed points
of the land, into a whine. She felt its savagery cut deeper
and deeper to her throat. She had pinned the sacks across
her chest, above her scarf, but the wind drove down into
the hollow bones of her body and then bitterly through
it, as if nothing was there.

When they put her to bed that night she was screaming
of Mitchy. She was lightheaded in the illusion that
Mitchy was at the bottom of a pit, laughing up at her.
She was terrified of the gangling legs, the green-mold hat,
the crab's eyes pressing back through the black-rimmed
spectacles. In exhaustion her body leaped in enormous
involuntary shudders of coldness that set her coughing.

"Well, you wanted work," Mrs. Wainwright said. "Are
y'above bein' seen with a truck?"

Always, at the back of Mrs. Wainwright's mind, had
seemed to lurk an impression that in some testing moment of crisis, such as this, Bella would not be strong
enough. Now there was the shadow of a hint that she
would not soil her hands.

"I didn't know I was above anything."

A moment of antagonism seemed to shoot up between
them, flare and die away. It might have risen, on Mrs.
Wainwright's side, from the bitterness of a notion that
bad luck never came singly: from a feeling that, as if
times were not hard enough and bad enough already,
sickness now had to take away a pair of hands.

Grimly she challenged:

"Somebody's got to do it."

"I'll do it," Bella said.

Harshly and stoically Mrs. Wainwright seemed to stare into the future, calculating and anticipating its growing shadow.

"Not as you need worry," she said. "The rate we're going on it won't last for long."

It lasted all winter. By day, if there was work, she traveled with the truck. At night she slept on the floor of the bedroom; or she lay awake, listening to the racked breathing of Nell, fighting rheumatic fever. Earlier, downstairs, the Wainwrights sat most of the evening in the kitchen, by the light of a single candle in a bright tin holder. Washing dried and aired on lines hung across the ceiling. A big wooden clothes horse was set up, filled mostly with thick flannel working shirts, beside a fire of slack, potato parings and cabbage stalks. Wainwright smoked pipes of tobacco made of coltsfoot leaves, which burned with a crude, dusky herbal smell. The pipe never drew very well and he tapped it constantly out on the fire-back. The walls of the little houses were so thin that it was possible to hear the people next door, the Pettits, stabbing at their fire-back, so that sometimes, as Mrs. Wainwright said, "it's a wonder you don't get the poker in your eye." That winter also Wainwright spent more time at evening prayer meetings and one result was that he shaved more often. Instead of shaving on Wednesdays and Saturdays he often shaved on Tuesdays, Thursdays,

Saturdays and Sundays, a fact that gave his long bony face a scoured, hungrier, more cadaverous air.

But sometimes there were pairs to be done quickly, and Wainwright, Con and Matty worked on past midnight. Half the night, in her bedroom, she lay listening to the grating of Nell's breathing and the echo, from the shop, of the flat sound of hammers. Sometimes when she got up in the darkness of January mornings the single lamp in the shop was still burning. And once when she went to collect the shoes Matty was still there, asleep across the bench, a file still in his hand, his mouth gaping like an upper.

Some days before this happened she was startled by something. She was waiting outside a factory in Addington when she saw a man run quickly into a factory fifty yards away, on the opposite side of the street. The factory, a converted chapel, had a double flight of stone steps outside it. A thin iron railing went up each side. And something about the way the man slid his hands quickly up the railing and gave it a casual parting flick at the top stiffened her coldly where she stood.

"Arch Wilson," she thought. "That was Arch Wilson."

She crossed the street and stood by the steps. She was trembling. A dry wind was blowing, drifting old papers into corners, where they were suddenly lifted in gray spirals of dust. One spiral spurted into a column that bore upwards a sheet of newspaper and slapped it against the railings. It remained pressed there by the force of wind and the railings showed through it like dark ribs through a quivering skin.

She was still watching the sheet of paper throbbing in the wind when the door slammed open and the man came out, darting down the steps on the opposite side. Before she was aware of it she called, "Arch! Arch Wilson!" and at the sound of the name he stopped and turned.

It was the same kind of friendly mealy-lipped face, under the same kind of healthy golden mustache, that she saw turned to her; but suddenly she knew she had made a mistake for a second time. She lifted both hands to her face with the shock of surprise and embarrassment. Then he grinned and swept a hand across the mustache and said:

"You calling me? What name?"

"It's nothing. It's all right. I made a mistake," she said.

He grinned. She was trembling. She could see white healthy teeth shining fresh as seeds in the thick red pod of his mouth. His hand made easy play on the steely curve of the rail. The fingers were muscular and golden-haired. The hands might have been the hands of Arch Wilson, lazily playing with the air of a summer afternoon.

"Looking for anything?" he said. "Out occasioning?"

Occasioning: the shoemaker's word for work-hunting, for what she was doing — touting, begging, hoping, hanging in alleyways and about the doors of factories for whatever they would throw out to her. She was aware of being a beggar asking for crumbs and suddenly she hated it. She hated the word, the mealy way it was muttered at her, the easy play of the hands. She hated the scrubby windy little town of high asphalt causeways and yellow alleyways where she ran like a beggar with a truck. The pride that had made her toss her head at Arch Wilson and say of her own shining dark eyes, "They're green — they're all green when you talk to me," and had later made her tie back her hair with a shoelace suddenly sprang to life again and made her aloof and cool and drawn up, like a tall girl, as she moved away.

"Whyn't you come down to my place?" he said. "I might find you a few pair."

She did not answer. She seemed to sail back across the street, wind-borne, stiff with pride, to where she had left the truck. She heard him laugh. It was so like the thick malty laugh of Arch Wilson that she turned round, surprised, to take a final look.

As he turned she saw the fresh-haired handsome mouth laugh again. With a start she realized that it was not the face, after all, that she hated. There was something tremendously compelling about the face. She wanted to look at the face. In its warm fleshy way it seemed to feel at her through a distance of fifty or sixty yards. Uneasily and subtly it seemed to get closer to her as she moved away.

Then as she seized the truck and began running he called:

"Whip behind! Whoop!" and she wanted to laugh suddenly in the full easy way she had laughed whenever Arch Wilson had joked with her, in that same way, by the sea.

She was aware, after that, of a new fear. She was afraid that suddenly there would be a day when she would turn a corner and be faced again with a mouth that laughed like that: Arch Wilson's mouth, the clean white teeth shining in the thick red pod of it, the fiery reddish-gold points of the mustache sparking above. She would see it and run past it; she would run away from it and want to look back. It would say some word to her that she hated; a word that would make her cheap; and then some word that mocked and fascinated and set her laughing.

Two days later she found Matty asleep on the bench in the shop. The little stove had gone out in the night. When she woke him he looked at her distantly, with eyes like frozen gray-blue pebbles. All the knuckles of his hands stood up arched and yellow with cold and for some time she stood by the bench and rubbed them with her hands.

"Don't you know where you are?"

"I know where I wish I wasn't," he said.

"Come on now. You want some tea now —"

"I wish I wasn't here," he said. He began trying to comb his shrunken fingers through his hair. "I'm awake enough to know that."

The fingers trying to comb their way through his hair had no feeling. Again, for a few minutes, she rubbed them with her hands. As she did so she remembered the day when, so shyly, he had spoken of making shoes for her and when the blood of his fingers had ticked against her own.

[133]

"You'll have to get to bed at night," she began saying, "or you'll end where Nell is —"

Suddenly he went to the door and slipped the wooden peg into place above the latch. He stood with his back to the door and started speaking. He was still so cold that she actually heard his teeth begin to chatter, like shaken nails.

"I'm going," he said. "I'm getting out. I'm all packed up. I was going last night. I was going to walk to Nenborough and get the night train. I must have dropped off. But I'm all packed — I'm ready, I'm going."

"Where?"

"London."

"London? You don't belong there."

"They'll be something there," he said. "A big place like that. There must be something for a good craft there. If not I'll get back to Birmingham. I went there once. I got the money. I been saving. I'm sick of this —"

"It'll be better in the spring. It'll right itself in the spring."

"Not for me," he said.

"Oh! no," she said. "Don't go. That's not right for you —"

"Would you come with me?" he said. "I been wanting to ask you. Come with me."

"What? — just like that, the two of us?"

"I don't care what they say." Cold seemed to have shrunken his entire body. He leaned small and beaten and compressed against the door. Now and then his teeth still chattered, to give his words an awful stuttering sound. "I can't stand it here much longer. Like this. Not much longer."

"When are you going?"

"Tonight perhaps. Tomorrow anyway."

Too readily, sorry for him, she was suddenly making her mistake of being too easy:

"I'll see. I'll have to see. I'll have to think it over."

Then she remembered the man she had mistaken for Wilson on the steps of the factory. She remembered the earlier mistake about Wilson by the river. She knew she was afraid of Wilson. She was afraid of coming face to face again with the easy, persuasive, laughing mouth.

"I got money. You needn't worry about that. I got plenty for both of us."

Then she remembered not only her fear and hatred of Wilson but her fear and hatred of waiting like a beggar on factory steps. That, in a way, she hated more than Wilson: the touting and cadging, the hoping and waiting.

She heard his body shudder. It actually shook the door. He tried to hold it still with his hands. Then it shook again, beating the thin loose panels with a rattle against the frame.

"You're cold," she said. "You're terribly cold."

His body gave its second leaping shudder. In pity she seized and held it in her arms. The bones of his face were stiff and she drew his head down and pressed it against her shoulder.

Daylight unfroze itself at the windows. She remembered the spider caught and suspended darkly among its cobwebs. And suddenly she felt it run again, in the form of her hatred and fear of Wilson, across her mind.

She said quickly, too readily again, too easy:

"I'll come. Don't worry. I'll come with you."

He tried to give a cold bony smile of gratitude.

"When? Tonight?"

"Tomorrow," she said. "One more day. You ought to sleep tonight."

He tried to smile a second time, his face excruciating and coldly vacant.

"I always wanted you to come," he said, "only I was frightened to ask you. I was frightened the others would know."

"They'll have to know."

"Why?"

His eyes were full of steely shyness.

"Because they must. Because I'll tell them."

"I thought we could go off without that."

"No," she said. "No."

"It'd be easier."

"I know it would be easier." Daylight unfroze gray and sunless beyond the cobwebs. A second dark impression of a running spider of fear made her cold too. She straightened the creased lapels of his jacket. "But I couldn't do that. I couldn't do that to anybody. I couldn't deceive anybody."

She took his cap from the peg behind him. She opened

the door and the light of morning came in full in her face.

"I never deceived anybody in my life," she said. "And I won't start with you."

But that day, over dinner, and again at teatime, in the light of the candle, she found it hard to say what she wanted to say. In the shop, moved by his coldness, his shaking and his distress, it had been easy to hold him and let pity, in warm and ready impulses, say what she wanted to say. But in the kitchen, pressed round by the faces of the Wainwrights, it was not so easy as that. It was not easy to look up, face them and say:

"I'm going away. I'm going with Matty."

And all winter, since Nell's illness, there had been something more than watchfulness on the Wainwright faces at meal tables. Each of them sat listening for a signal from Nell. The girl kept a walking stick at her bedside and whenever she wanted anything she rapped with low, dropping signals on the floor. These tappings arrested the little kitchen dramatically into silences. The taps were no louder, sometimes, than the drips of a water tap and occasionally a single one, like a final gathering drop, came so long after the others that it was like an echo.

That day, at teatime, it seemed to Bella that suddenly Nell began rapping.

"I'll go," she said and as she got up too nervously and too quickly to slip through the stairs door she caught on the face of Matty an expression of acute appeal that was matched by one of surprise, almost alarm, on the face of Con.

"She must be hearing things," Mrs. Wainwright said.

"I heard it," Matty said.

Upstairs, in the bedroom, she started nervously putting her things into a cardboard box. There had been no rap from Nell. The only light in the room was the reflection from the street lamp outside and in the frosty green cast of it the girl turned her face from the bed.

"What are you doing?"

"I'm putting a few things together."

"Things?"

"Just a few things."

"You're going with Matty," the girl said. "I know. He told me."

She began crying: weakly, without sound, her mouth covered with the sheets. Bella bent down, laid her own head on the pillow and said:

"You'll be better without me. You'll have more room. And then the work. I only half pull my weight here."

"I don't want you to go. Matty went once before and came back again."

"I'll come back."

"You won't. I know you won't. And anyway I don't think I'll see you if you do. I've been laying so long here — "

Under the window was a tiny space of garden, four

yards square, between the front parlor and the street.
Bella got up from the bed. She opened the window and
dropped the cardboard box on the frosty earth outside.
From the bed the girl cried with a low quiet flood of
tears and Bella wanted to say "Don't tell anybody. I
wanted to tell them myself but somehow I couldn't," and
she kissed the sweat-cold face instead.

An hour later there was a moment, with Mrs. Wainwright upstairs and Wainwright already off to a prayer
meeting and Matty already gone and Con, as she thought,
in the shop, when she was alone in the little kitchen. She
grabbed her coat quickly and put it on. She pushed a
hunk of bread into the pocket and went outside.

It was starry and cold as she ran through the yards.
She picked up the cardboard box from the garden in the
street. She could see frost in brilliant circular prints forming everywhere on the black pavement under the street
lamps and she began to run on the road for fear of falling down.

The branch-line station was at the north end of the
town: a small terminus with a single row of four gas
lamps down the slope of the yard outside and two more
lamps, one at each end, on the footbridge that spanned
the line. She noticed that one of the lights on the bridge
was not working. Then as she went past it Con darted
suddenly out from under the curve of the bridge frame-
work and caught her by the coat and held her so that she
could not run.

"You're not going."

"Let me go. Who says so?"

"I say so. You're not going — "

"Who told you? Who told you?"

"Nell," he said. "Nell told me yesterday."

She heard the engine of a train shunting in the yards. The pitch of the road below the bridge was too low for her to see the station. She heard only the harsh cough of the engine as it shunted, the drag and clink of a coupling on frosty air somewhere in the darkness down the line.

Then she heard the engine coming up the line. She could only think of it as the train she wanted. She started struggling and dropped the cardboard box containing her things. He kicked it away and held her closer under the skeleton of the bridge. Then she started struggling again:

"I got to go. Matty's waiting. I got to go. Let me go. Matty's waiting — "

"He can wait. Let him wait," he said.

"I promised. I want to go. I got to go. I promised — "

"The train's coming," he said.

The train came slowly up from the yards. She heard a signal behind it clatter up to safety in the hard still night air. Smoke and steam rushed up and hit the roof of the bridge and enveloped it. She was caught in a sulphury damp warm cloud, the gush of train-smell rising all about her, and she started struggling again as doors up and down the platform opened and banged.

"What will Matty think? I promised." It hurt her more than anything to feel that she had promised. "I prom-ised — "

"He shouldn't make you promise. That's his fault. He'd got no right to make you."

"I got a right. I got a right to go if I want to —"

"Not now," he said.

She heard suddenly the shriek of a whistle and the harsh indrawn breath of the engine as it moved away. She was stung to the verge of tears as she thought of Matty sitting alone in a carriage, under the bowl of naked yellow gas flares. With fierceness she moved her head and looked up and saw train smoke clearing from a sky of intense blackness filled with quivering frosty gas-green stars. She felt herself quiver too and said:

"What will he think of me? I promised. I hate that — promising and then —"

"He knew you weren't going."

"Knew?"

"I told him."

Incredibly, in bewilderment, she turned her face again, staring up at him. He was still holding her with both arms and in the darkness under the bridge she was so close to him that it was hard to see his face.

"I told him you wouldn't go."

"You told him! — Why? — What did he say?"

"Matt's all right," he said. "He didn't say much. He never does." And then, after a pause:

"He knows I want you."

In amazement she had nothing to say. In stunned dreaminess she stood with him there for a long time, echo after echo of the words dropping down inside herself: "He knows I want you. He knows I want you. He knows I want you."

He did not speak much more. He did not attempt to kiss her. It was so cold that once when she moved her hand she could feel the rough shell of hoarfrost forming like a crust, almost as thick as snow, on the iron of the bridge, but she hardly noticed it. "He knows I want you," she kept thinking. "He knows I want you."

Some long time later he moved and unclasped her. He felt of her hands and said:

"You're cold. Your hands are cold."

In fresh amazement she saw him suddenly climb half-way up the trellised ironwork of the bridge, reaching up to where the lamp was.

"What are you doing?" she said. "Con! — what are you doing?"

She heard the clink of the lamp chain as he pulled it down. And as light flooded down on the bridge and illuminated the balustrade, the steps and the trellis of the sides with the green-white flare of frost, she saw him smile: a curious downcast rancorless smile, untriumphant, that had in it the beginnings of what she was to know presently as something more remarkable than gentleness.

"I put it out," he said. "It's time I put it on again."

VIII

SPRING came too early, false with bursts of blue warmth in March, a bright glinting on brooks and river and a few first spare primroses in copses southward of the town after late falls of snow.

"I saw a brimstone on the shop wall," Con said. Mrs. Wainwright dreamed aloud an occasional thought on the cuckoo. "Ah! when we get the cuckoo a-coming to pick the dirt up," was her old, eternal infallible prayer for spring. "Get the cuckoo here," she would say, "and very like we'll have Nell on her feet again."

Most days the elderly doctor stumped through the sacred front door and up the narrow stairs and into the little front bedroom without any warning of himself except the thump of a thorn stick on the bare treads of the stairs. He wore a high squarish gray derby hat. He had side whiskers like distinguished gray lamb cutlets. In diagnosis or examination he put on a pair of pince-nez that successfully concealed, in the remote gray eyes, all sign of whatever he was thinking. It was safe to suppose that if he stumped upstairs and down again within two minutes there was no change in the condition of the patient or that he had nothing to say about it if there was. If he chose to speak at all it was with the reluctant gruffness of a not unamiable dog trained solely to repeat a few monosyllables. Only crisis could incite him to sentences.

On a day in April he actually put his head into the kitchen and barked:

"Someone to go up to the surgery at once. I'm going that way. I can give a lift," and then withdrew without waiting or explanation.

As Bella drove back with him in his brown dogcart to his long flat-fronted stucco house on the market square he actually spoke another word or two. The sun was soft on the grayish yellow stone of the old tall houses of the square. The buds of chestnuts were varnished bright bronze, with strokes of emerald. The doctor said:

"Treacherous. Treacherous weather. I don't trust it. We must watch your sister very carefully."

His mistake in thinking that Nell was her sister touched and stirred and alarmed her. She did not think of contradicting it.

And when Nell died, three days later, it was very much as if she had lost a sister. It drew her closer to Con.

The day of the funeral was a warm blue hard day, bright with dancing flies, almost summery with heat and sun. Lost and blind, Wainwright groped through the house with shovels of coal, backing up fires that had never needed to be lighted. The little parlor, with sun pouring in at the south window, steamed like a hothouse. In the false spring sultriness the bump of the descending coffin was like the sound of a beating pump and Mrs. Wainwright's voice was a black dry dirge:

"Easter an' all," she said. "Easter an' all."

Bleakly the words, like her prayer for the cuckoo, went bitterly and inconsolably through everything she said that day and for some long time afterwards. Her bitterness was the bitterness born of cheating. Spring had promised and spring had cheated: spring had taken away. It would have been better if winter had killed with a dark clean cold cut. But the treachery of spring, with its brimstone falsely enticed, the spare too-early primroses, the promise of the cuckoo that would pick up the stale sour dirt of winter, was something she could not bear. She could not be reconciled. Inevitably, in death, there had to be a villain and for some time, in Nell's death, Mrs. Wainwright saw it as the spring.

After an afternoon crowded with distant and sometimes strange relatives drinking great quantities of tea in the kitchen and the parlor Bella found herself standing on the ash path of the garden with Con. She stood looking down at a solitary daffodil, green-cased that morning, that had opened like a full yellow-green skirt in the heat of the day. She stooped to smell it and it was possible to breathe all spring and even a hint of summer in the free warm odor of the single flower.

"Couldn't we walk somewhere?" she said. "I got so stifled and so hot in there. I'd like to walk somewhere."

"We could walk as far as the Fox Coverts," he said. "There'll be a few primroses there."

She remembered Con calling to his mother that they would be back inside an hour. It was dry and dusty on the footpath, cracked from the drought of spring, as they walked southeastward out of the town. There was a touch or two of full green, brilliant and fresh as parsley, on the crests of hawthorn hedges and a few white stars of blossom on leafless boughs of blackthorn. Everywhere in the spring heat there was a great throbbing of thrush-song and over on the big dry wheatfields a background of larks that went shrilling higher and higher into the blue above the tender curves of corn.

"It seemed queer without Jedd and Matty there," he said.

There had been neither leave for Jedd, bound by spring exercises at Salisbury, nor an address from Matty. "And ain't likely to be," Mrs. Wainwright said, "so long as he's living hand to mouth. That's like him. He'll let us know fast enough when he's doing well. But Jedd," she said bitterly. "I don't say so much about Matty — but you'd think they could do 'ithout one soldier for a day. You'd ha' thought they could ha' spared me Jedd."

It was so hot that Bella took off her coat as she walked. From the Fox Coverts, high up on flattish land, on the extreme far tip of the escarpment above the valley, it was possible to see the spires of nine churches, like pale stone swords. On the edges of the Coverts the stalks of primroses were already long and pink and hairy in the sun. A tip or two of scarlet burned on larch boughs. A few trembling anemones, like white bells, were scattered about the broken dancing shade.

Some time after they had gathered primroses, with purple violets and a few occasional white ones, fat and pure as snowdrop buds, and a few anemones, they spread her coat on the edge of the spinney and sat down. From time to time she put the flowers to her face. She drew at the dark violet scent of them and at the soft flat primroses with their airier lighter breath. Finally she lay down, her hands underneath her head, and looked at the sky.

"There still isn't a cloud," she said. "There hasn't been a cloud all day."

She could hear a thousand larks singing all down through the valley. Behind her, in the spinney of young ash boughs and red-tipped larch and hazel, there was a great belling chorus of thrushes. She shut her eyes and heard him say:

"The sun's still hot on your face. You look quite hot with just lying there."

"I feel I haven't lain in the sun for years," she said. "For a terrible long time."

She drew her arms from underneath her head and stretched them upwards like a person stretching after a doze. Her eyes were still shut: it was like a strange and miraculous coincidence when she found her arms folding about his shoulders. The darting pleasure of it made her give a little gasp. Like lying in the sun, like the dark scent of violets and the chorus of larks, it was a final positive sensation of waking.

When he began kissing her it was like a moment both of them had been waiting for. She drew him down hungrily. She could feel her skin running with little darting fires that had never run there since a moment she had lain with Arch Wilson by the sea, among prickly thorns of sea thistle, on a summer afternoon.

Everything she had not been able to give to Jedd or Matty or even Con himself came rushing up inside her in a generous and intoxicating mass of joy and hungriness, with a touch of tears. When she opened her eyes again she lay staring softly at him in wonder.

"You look as if you've never seen me before."

"That's how I feel," she said.

"The same Con," he said.

"No," she said.

"How am I different?"

"All of you," she said. "Or perhaps it's me that's changed."

She felt wonder grow and expand inside her with such delicacy that she did not want to speak again. She heard him say:

"You were changing all the time. I could see that — "

Suddenly she thought: "If you ask me all about it I'll tell you. I'll tell you why I came here. Arch Wilson and everything. All of it. I want to tell you. You only have to ask. I never told anyone in my life but I'll tell you now."

But when she opened her eyes again she saw on his face a look of such extraordinary happiness that she knew there was not a thought of it in his mind.

"I remember the time when I didn't know if I liked you," she said. "You were so fiery and quick. Like that day in the harvest field."

"I frightened myself that day."

"Don't let's talk about it," she said. "Hear the larks — can you hear them? They must be singing all the way from here to the sea."

With another rush of joy and hunger she laughed and held him to her again. She felt a quivering flash of his turning body. Agonized and happy and in growing wonder she thought:

"Do you know what you do to me? Do you know what it's like to feel like this? After all that time? — "

The sun went down across the valley. Beyond the stone swords of nine church spires it set fire to a sky that for a long time smoldered with bronze and orange and a far high glow of pale pure spring green. Under twilight the smell of spring earth warmed by sun seemed to thicken all along the copse edge. As she looked up she could have sworn that the fiery tips of the larches had lengthened since late afternoon. Even after the sun had gone down and the branches were black again in the clear blue spring twilight she could hear the one exposed voice of a thrush whistling madly against darkness and the thin pure echo of a solitary lark in the field below.

She did not know what time it was as they began to

walk slowly back again. As she looked up at the thrilling particles of spring stars and felt the soft too-warm spring night air on her face she thought again, as she had done once with Jedd, that the moment was too perfect and she herself too happy.

"We shouldn't be so happy," she said. "I mean today. With Nell and everything. It doesn't seem right that we should."

"Let's take her the flowers," he said.

When they got to the cemetery the entrance gates were locked. Iron railings and a cinder path went down the boundary on one side and halfway along it Con climbed over and then lifted her down inside.

The stiff hummock of clay where Nell lay was fresh yellow under starlight. A few bunches of flowers, daffodils, winter stocks and blood wall-flowers, lay at either end. She saw him kneel down and put their own flowers in the center of the mound of clay. In a suspense of love for him and pity for Nell she felt again that she could not bear the moment and she said:

"Hold me a moment. Hold on to me — just a moment — in case I float away."

He held her with speechless tenderness. He kissed her once or twice and touched her hair. She had nothing to say except once, in quiet wonder "So many stars. I never saw so many stars," and felt once again that she was all lightness herself under the light of them. In his new suspense of entrancement she felt him run his fingers through the dark thickness of hair and she said:

"When you do that to me I feel you all over. I feel your hands inside me, going deep down."

It was past eleven o'clock when they went into the kitchen, going in quietly, in a sort of after-spell, to find Mrs. Wainwright sitting by the fireless stove in candle-light, her candle-colored hands laid out on the black slope of her lap.

"So you thought you would come back."

"We took a few flowers for Nell," Con said. "A few primroses we got — "

"I count she'd got flowers a-new," she said, "'ithout you traipsin' off half the night, looking for any more."

Bella began to say: "We just wanted — " and then stopped. It was suddenly no use. It was useless and impossible to explain how the two of them had felt out there: the wild singing of larks across the valley, the glow of stars, the pity the two of them felt for a sister, the inexplicable sensation of suspense and floating away.

"Your Dad's been in bed this two hours or more. And me with nothing to do but sit here and let the fire look black at me."

"You could have gone up."

"H'm," she said, "and lay there a-wonderin' all night who's running away with who this time?"

"Good night," Bella said.

Her tears were acid and blinding as she went upstairs. She was too distraught to undress and she lay down on her bed as she was. She lay for a long time crying, the suspense inside herself broken, the youth in her jabbed

and wounded again, her mind dark and bruised. Then
she was aware of Con in the room, kneeling against the
bed.

"I couldn't sleep. I knew you were crying somehow,"
he said. "Don't cry —"

"That was a terribly cruel, bitter thing to say to me."

"She never meant it. She's not herself."

"That was herself — that's the way she speaks. That's
the way she's always speaking. That's what she thinks of
me."

He kissed her face. "You'll be cold, lying here like
this —"

"How else would I feel?" she said, "but cold? — After
what she said to me?"

He put his arms completely round her, drawing her up
to him. "It'll be all over and forgot tomorrow." He was
speaking very softly, in a whisper, and she realized that
there was no anger in him, no rancor, no more of the old
aggressive flaring self.

"It was so wonderful out there," she said. "I never
thought that could happen to us. And then she had to
break it."

From outside the bedroom the catch of a door made a
snap in the darkness. A sound of feet on bare linoleum
rustled like sharply crumpled paper. Harshly Mrs. Wainwright called out:

"You needn't think I never heard you a-creepin' and
a-shufflin' along there. Because I did. Ain't your own bedroom big enough now 'ithout you must go into her'n?"

There was something else she could not hear. She felt his body give a tremendous start. The anger she felt had been extinguished came flaming back.

"Don't answer! Don't answer!" she said. "Don't go! Don't answer!"

As she pressed his face against her body she could feel his mouth sobbing with pulses of rage. Outside, on the landing, a sound of feet rustled away and Mrs. Wainwright said:

"As if we ain't had enough today. As if we ain't had we bellyful on it today, buryin' her — "

She heard him in another rush of rage grinding his teeth in the darkness. It was a terrible sound. She rocked him to and fro.

"Don't let it do that to you. Don't let it do that — not like that again. Let it just go out of your mind. I've got you — let it go out of your mind."

For some time longer she held him there against the bed. After a time she said "It was wonderful out there in the spinney. With the primroses. And the larks and the violets. Think of that. Not what she said. That doesn't matter," and gradually she felt him calming down.

Until at last he was able to say:

"I'll go back now. But she can say what she likes and it'll never get you away from me. Not what she says, or anybody else. Not what she does or what she thinks or anything. It'll never get you away from me."

"Go to sleep now," she said with new tenderness. She kissed his face like the face of a child that has distressed itself beyond sleeping. "Think of the things we did."

Inconsolably, without demonstration, all through springtime, Mrs. Wainwright grieved for Nell. She sat for long periods in the small front parlor, staring at the street. On Sundays she walked with Wainwright or Con as far as the cemetery, dumbly placed a few flowers on the mound and then without a word walked back again. There was never, during all this time, a word or a moment of open distress. Her face had something of the look of an extinguished and half-burned candle, compressed and colorless, with a thin wick of hair tied at the top, its flesh bloodless and waxen.

Inside herself, twisted, she lived an agony of self-reproaches. Spring had promised; spring had suddenly taken away. She conceived that she ought, in some way she could not define, to have been able to do something about the spring. In a blunted and groping fashion she castigated herself with a notion that she ought to have let the living, the healthy, look after themselves. Too much and too often she had withheld herself from the sick.

Gradually spring, rainy and cool after the false beautiful bursts of March, ceased to be a villain who had promised, tricked and taken away. Her bitterness against it became assuaged by the fact that at last it had belied itself. With grim triumph she pointed out its defection.

"I knew it could never last," she said. "I knew we should have to suffer."

Now, too, there was work again; the factories were running. There was no longer any need to tout across the valley. The thing that had killed Nell was behind them again, but it too rankled, another source of bitterness, that she could not forget.

And soon her grief, shut down inside herself with her grievances, unexpressed, not only grew big and sour. It began to turn itself on Bella — Bella who had laughed too much with Jedd, Bella who had been too ready to run away with Matty, Bella who had taken the place of Nell. And finally, mostly, and most of all, Bella who was in love with Con.

At first it was not merely that she was jealous of love. Through the vision of grief she saw it as ridiculous. "It urges you to see 'em. It makes you sick the way they look and sit there." And if Wainwright, patient and consolatory, said "I knowed the time when you looked like that," she had nothing but the cold flare of disgust in answer:

"Not me you never did. That I do know. Not a-maundering and a-mooning like they do."

"You ought to be glad about it," Wainwright said. "When folks are happy you ought to be glad for them."

"Happy!" she said.

"It's not Christian to feel like you do," he said. "It's not Christian to hate people."

"And who said anything about hating? I never said I hated nobody. It just urges you, that's all, it just urges you to death!"

"Mother, Mother," he would say to her, "that's not the way."

Then gradually, since she was jealous of love and since her way of looking at it through grief was as near hatred as ever mattered, antagonism became an obsession. Bella became not only the villain replacing the falsity of spring. She became a canker, eating at Mrs. Wainwright's mind.

And perhaps it was natural that the canker seemed more odious because it had become more beautiful. It was not simply that when she wore her black necklace and black earrings and the black shoes with the swallow buckles that she looked prettier and more striking; or that she had recovered, in her way of walking, the pride that made her look so much taller than she was. Her face was alive and fresh and almost painfully happy under its curling mass of young black hair. Her lips had a way of parting spontaneously, fresh-colored, with a tender flowering that was more wonderful because she did not seem to be aware, most of the time, that it was there.

"She'll be down in a minute, all dolled up," Mrs. Wainwright would say. "Scented to death. Earrings on. High and mighty."

Through grief she saw love and the pride of youth as monstrous irritations. She saw the arched flowering beauty of it as something contemptuous. She saw it, finally, as her means of losing Con.

"It'll wear off," she said. "She's that sort. Like a fly a-buzzin' and never settlin' for more'n a minute together.

She went for Jedd and Matty and now it's Con. It'll wear off. It won't last no time."

By the beginning of June the weather had settled again. After the late wet spring the drying silt of the valley began to feed the grasses. All the meadows became white with sweeps of moon-daisies that were like repeated Milky Ways. In the upper brooks, in iron-red marshes, cresses grew rapidly, dark and thick, and hawthorn turned pale pink and scattered itself on streams that were presently half hidden in elder flower and honeysuckle and arches of rose.

On a warm Saturday afternoon Con came into the kitchen with a basket of dark fresh cresses, and Mrs. Wainwright was swift to notice his boots.

"You stomped fur enough in for 'em, didn't you?" she said. "You're plastered up to your neck."

"You know how they grow up there. All in the marsh."

"You look as if you jumped in," she said.

In the sink he ran water onto the cresses. He was laughand happy inside himself as he washed them. He could not tell her that he had been leaping from island to island of sedge, chased by Bella, and had slipped and fallen in. A brood of young wild duck had risen just in front of him at the sound of his hands slapping into marsh water, and then Bella had fallen too. He had not laughed so much for a long time. His chest was quite painful with laughter as the two of them lay for the rest of the afternoon on a stretch of higher ground, in the sun, drying themselves, watching the green skein of young duck cir-

cling round and round the marsh with its pink boun-
daries of May blossom bleaching and fading against a pure
June sky.

"And where's she got to?"

He could not tell the truth of that either. He simply
swilled the cresses in the sink and said:

"She's gone to buy a handkerchief or two. She lost one
across the fields somewhere."

"I'd ha' thought she'd have had handkerchiefs a-new
'ithout wastin' more money. It don't come so easy, do'st?"

"It's my money," he said. "I give it her."

"Ah! and you'll very like wish you'd kept it in your
pocket," she said, "afore you're that much older."

He drained water from the cresses. Microscopically she
peered into the washed leaves with their fine white ten-
drils of root.

"Wash 'em well, wash 'em well," she said. "I don't call
that washed yit."

"Where's Dad?" he said.

"It's Saturday afternoon, ain't it? You know where he
is. Or should do."

For two or three hours on Saturday afternoons Wainwright cleaned and polished the plain altar brass of the
chapel; it was a kind of working penance that kept him
there till six.

"Well, she's either coming or she ain't," Mrs. Wainwright said. "Any road we'll start we teas and chance it."

They sat down to tea and home-baked bread and cresses.
In summer it was customary to sit with the door of the

kitchen open; but now suddenly she got up and shut it and said:

"I felt a draft round my back. The wind sits that way."

For ten minutes they crunched cresses, dipping them into salt. Sometimes she peered at a stalk and gave a grunt in her chest and picked out the dark grain of a thorn. Then she found a fleck of earth or a yellowed leaf and charged him again, tartly, with only half washing them. And it was with that same kind of grunt that she said:

"Buying the whole shop, seem'ly."

He was angered; he flicked water from a thick sprig of cresses and said:

"And what if she is? Keep on muttering."

"The more you give her the more she'll want, that's all."

"I know what she wants and I know what I'll give her," he said.

"Well," she said, "you may know some things."

He remembered what Bella had said — "Don't answer! Don't answer! Let it go out of your mind! Don't answer!" — and he sat there silent, staring in front of him, dabbing cresses into salt.

"But I'll tell you one thing you don't know."

"Ah?" he said. "What?"

He licked salt from his lips; he let it lie on the tip of his tongue, giving sharpness to it after the single word.

Her small eyes were already narrowed. A half-circle of thinnest wrinkles, like crow's feet, stretched across the flat side-bones of her forehead. They appeared in the same way, sharper, more grimly reduced, about her mouth, and she said:

"You know why she come here? In the fust place? You know what was the matter with her?"

"She was half dead. I know that," he said.

"Half dead and no wonder."

"Give me another cup," he said.

She poured tea. He saw a little cloud of iridescent steam hang above his cup as he took it from her. He felt the sides of the cup very hot, almost scalding, on his fingers. He waited.

And then she was speaking. Tersely it was out at last: the trouble she was in, the baby, the long walk, the man she was after.

"You never knowed that, did you? But I knew and Nell knew."

In a surprise of thought, unsavage, he had nothing to say. He dabbed cresses into salt. His only sign of agitation was to commit what was for her the unpardonable sin of drinking with his mouth full, of washing down half-bitten cresses with a great gulp of tea.

"That'll tell you summat about her. That'll tell you what sort she is."

He gripped the cup. He felt the scalding sides of it penetrate his fingers with pain. He felt that in another second he would lift it and throw the tea in her face. But for the space of perhaps twenty seconds or so he sat poised on the edge of a single naked nerve, fighting himself and fighting not to move.

Then in the moment when he felt the nerve break and he could hold himself no longer he heard footsteps in the yard outside. He saw her glance quickly at the door. He grasped then, for the first time, why she had shut it.

In that moment, for the only time, she could not face him. She got up to reach for the kettle where it stood on the stove.

In another moment the door opened and Bella stood there with a parcel in her hands.

"Was I long?" she said. "Did you wait? You didn't wait tea for me, did you?"

"It was ready and we started," he said.

Her eyes were shining. He saw her lips parting themselves spontaneously, eager and laughing:

"I got it! I got the one I wanted!"

"Got what?" Mrs. Wainwright said.

"The dress," she said. She looked straight at him and he could not speak; he could not bear to see her, he thought, so full of happiness. "The green one — the one you saw. The one you wanted."

"What next?" Mrs. Wainwright said.

At seven o'clock that evening he was still waiting for her to come downstairs. He had tied and retied his necktie half a dozen times or more before the pier glass. His father was shaving at the sink, scraping with slow sandstone strokes at a three-day beard. His mother was sitting in the front parlor. He knew that if she did not emerge from it in time she would still be able to see himself and Bella, in the street outside, as they walked away.

But at the last moment, as Bella's footsteps sounded on the stairs, the situation was too much for her. She came through to the kitchen. She fussed with an airing shirt of Wainwright's that hung above the stove.

She was still turning the shirt as Bella came into the kitchen. The starched front of it gave a crackle in her hands. She did not speak. For as many years as she could remember she had worn, on Sundays, a dark gray dress, severe, almost black, and with it a black hat whose trimmings she sometimes changed. On Sunday nights the dress was folded, put away, moth-balled and not touched again till Sunday. In time, perhaps, if they lived and had good luck, as her guarded phrase went, she might buy herself another. If that happened the Sunday dress would become a Saturday dress; the Saturday dress would become a weekday dress, for evenings or afternoons. The dress for Saturday and the dress for Sunday could not be interchanged, any more than Wainwright could pray with Methodists in the morning and cross the road to sing at the meeting of Baptists at night. Her Sunday dress had been a new dress when Matty was a boy and she remembered how, for some weeks, she had not dared to wear it because it seemed too new and too precious and because there was never a Sunday that seemed quite beautiful enough.

For a moment or two a splash of Wainwright's lather falling into the sink was the only sound as Bella stood in

the kitchen, wearing the new green dress. It might have
been a spit of impatience or disgust from Mrs. Wainwright herself and its echo was another crackle in the
front of the shirt.

She still did not speak; but Wainwright, half-lathered,
white razor steaming as he held it poised above the shaving mug, said:

"That's a new 'un, ain't it? Where did that come from?"

She said simply, with pride:

"Con bought it. He bought it for me."

"What color do they call that?" Wainwright said.

"It's a kind of sage," she said. She smoothed one hand
and then another down the opposite sleeves of the dress,
fingering the cuffs with their buttons of darker green.
"But it's brighter than that in the sun."

He stood with razor steaming and poised, the lather
drying on his chin. As he looked at her standing there, all
in green except for the black earrings, the black necklace
and a feathery black hat that was like a continuation of
her dark curly hair, he had a flash of remembrance about
her. He saw her as he had first seen her, under the street
lamp, her hair tied with a bootlace, staring in the snow.

And suddenly it gave him pride to think that he had
some part in bringing her there; and then because pride
was a bad thing he simply felt humility and happiness
about her. He could not help thinking that there was
something inevitable and preordained about the way he
had met her that night and given her comfort and brought
her home. It seemed so long ago and impossible now and

she looked so beautiful and fully awakened standing there that a touch of the old wag in him came back:

"Well: they never got theirselves up like that when I wor a young chap. Very like a good thing too."

She laughed. Across the front of the dress a few rows of buttons were repeated horizontally, narrowing down to the center of the bust. He gave a second chuckle, another gesture of waggishness with the careless open razor:

"What's that in the front? A bead frame?" He laughed at his face in the mirror, pleased with the joke he made. "Well, so long as Con's got summat to count on ——"

"You count what you're doing," Mrs. Wainwright said, "'ithout you want one less head to reckon."

But for once she could not suppress him; he was not to be subdued. Something of the youth in him, the careless robust young shoemaker who had roamed beerily about the countryside at prize fights and races and fairs and fox hunts, wild and flashy, came swaggering back:

"I like that color. It's a good deal like a young titty-bottle leaf. Don't you think so, Con?"

"It's the color he wanted," Bella said.

"Green," Mrs. Wainwright said. With a sort of scoffing crackle she laid the shirt in readiness for Wainwright on the edge of the corner copper. "I know folks as wouldn't be seen in it, not for love nor money."

"Old women!" Wainwright said. "Who takes any notice o' that? Who cares whether it's lucky or onlucky so long as it looks good? Who cares about old women's tales?"

"It's lucky for me," Bella said.

Mrs. Wainwright sniffed and said "H'm!" Then Wainwright said: "Summat smells nice too. Like a beanfield," and a moment later he waved them goodby through the little kitchen window, with a cheerful flash of his razor.

"You mind you don't cut your head off," Mrs. Wainwright said, and then went back into the parlor to catch a glimpse of the dress she hated.

For about an hour they walked along the towpath, downstream, through meadows that seemed, Con thought, even thicker and starrier with June daisies than when he had first brought her there. He was very quiet. It was too early for the first hay to be cut but across the water he could smell, in the sultry evening air, the scent of water mint and rose. The sun went down in a glow of pure brazen yellow, flaming on tall masses of uncut water flags; and then, in a backwater, beyond three poplars, on the unburst heads of water lilies and the new fresh bronze leaves.

"I keep thinking of the evening we first came up here," he said. "We had a boat because I thought you'd get too tired."

"I remember that," she said. "This is where you caught your butterflies."

He stopped under the poplars, in shadow. There was hardly any wind in the hot evening, but the leaves of the poplars were turning incessantly.

"There was something about you I didn't know then," he said.

"Me? About me?"

"About when you first came here," he said. He paused. "She told me." He spoke of his mother distantly, neutrally, with neither anger nor affection. "She told me this afternoon."

His effort to keep as calm as possible about his mother made the entire expression of his face seem flat. She looked up at it with a sudden sensation of fright. For a moment or two she felt the blood draining rapidly out of her own face and then slowly out of her legs and arms, leaving her trembling and chilled.

"About you and having the baby," he said.

She could not say anything.

"Was it Wilson?" he said.

"Yes."

As she spoke he stared in front of him. His eyes were slightly downcast as they fixed themselves on the unbroken buds of the water lilies under the poplar trees. It was impossible, for a few moments longer, to tell what he was thinking and almost in terror she said:

"Why did she tell you that? Does it make any difference?"

"She was mad about something — "

"Does it make any difference?"

She felt she wanted to scream the words. A great rush of air drove through the poplars, startling every leaf, and she said:

"Does it? Now? After all this time?"

"Yes," he said.

He seemed, she thought, to be turning away from her. She wanted to scream again and the water seemed to tilt, dark, then light, then quivering with poplar-shadow, all along the backwater.

A moment later he was holding her. He was speaking in a long rush of words, his mouth against her face.

"It does matter," she heard him say. "All the time I couldn't understand what was wrong with you. I never understood that. That way you used to go about. Half dead. That was what I could never understand."

"Oh! my God!" she said.

She felt herself slipping away into darkness. The rush of terror inside her seemed to turn completely over, like a struggling fish. She bit with her teeth into the shoulder of his jacket so that she should not scream and he said:

"It makes all the difference. I know what you meant now when you said 'Not yet. Not now.' That time I wanted to kiss you."

She cried almost tearlessly. A recollection of all the happiness of the afternoon flowered with it. It stabbed her with fresh joy. Then she was laughing and crying at the same time.

He laughed too. He put his fingers on the beadlike buttons across the front of her dress and said:

"You remember what you were going to do tonight?"

"No."

"You were going to learn me to dance," he said.

"Dance? So I was."

That, she remembered, was what the new dress was for.

She had been so happy in the afternoon that she had had a sudden feeling that she would like to dance somewhere: outside, perhaps, by the river, under chestnut trees. Then when he told her "I can't dance," she had said: "It wouldn't matter anyway. I've got no dress to dance in."

"Do you still feel like dancing?" he said.

"Do you?" she said. "After all that? After the things you know about me?"

He did not speak. She saw on his face an extraordinary look of happiness. It was clear and quiet. He looked at her for a long time, fingering the rows of buttons across her dress, and finally she said:

"What are you thinking? Nothing bad of me? I couldn't bear it if you thought anything bad of me."

"I'm counting," he said. She laughed and felt his hands pressing with great gentleness against her breasts, for the first time. "I've got something to count on now." He was smiling. "Do you still feel like dancing?"

"If you want to —"

"I do," he said. "If you think I could learn."

"You'll learn. It's easy," she said, and she felt that already her body was dancing under his hands.

They walked back to the pub. Two fiddles and a piano were playing in the long front bar. It was still hot, the windows were open and the sound of music floated down under the chestnut trees and away across the river. A trellis of larch poles made an archway from the side door of the pub to the gate by the bridge, and many roses were in bloom on it, heavy and full blown after the heat of the day. Hundreds of petals had fallen on the path in the glow of the windows like scattered pink and yellow spoons.

Because he was shy at first she took him down by the water, under the chestnut trees, thirty or forty yards away, to dance where nobody was. Most of the chestnut blossom had already fallen and faded but before the evening darkened completely a few pink and white drifts still shone on the river's edge among the reeds.

"Hold me like this," she said. "And with this hand, lightly, let yourself go — don't clutch me — lightly now, lightly — "

At first he was clumsy with the steps. He was afraid that someone would see him. In nervousness he kept laughing. A boat came into the landing-stage from upstream, rowed by a young man in a cream and red striped blazer and a girl in a white frock with a big yellow straw hat on her lap.

"Wait a minute. Wait," he said. "Wait till they've gone."

When the boat had been moored and the couple had gone and they were alone again she said:

"You're picking it up. You're doing well. It isn't easy dancing outside like this, on gravel. Next winter we could dance at the Assembly Rooms."

"Where did you learn to dance?" he said.

"Where I was," she said. "At the Three Bells. Before I came here."

"Did you ever dance with Wilson?"

"No," she said. "Never with him."

Presently she felt that her hat was in the way. She stopped dancing and unpinned it and laid it down by the bole of a chestnut tree. As she freed her hair and shook it out and straightened it a little with her hands she happened to glance up and see him standing there, two or three yards away, transfixed as he stared at her, grave in wonder. The green of her dress was deeper and brighter in the distant glow of the bar light than it had been in the evening sun. It gave her an effect of melting into the greenness under the chestnuts and the background of thick lilacs that marked the end of the garden at the water's edge.

A moment later he took two or three steps towards her. Then he was holding her there, hatless, against the trunk of the tree. Then he drew her round the trunk of the tree, into the shadow, and began kissing her.

He kissed her for a long time and by the end of it the music had stopped. She could hear the summer night silence singing away across miles of darkened meadows. From the garden she could smell the scent of a mock orange bush, overpowering and too-sweet, and with it all the lighter, purer breath of roses.

She felt herself float away on a stream of summer darkness. "Keep loving me," she thought. "Don't stop loving me. I couldn't bear it now if you stopped loving me." Then the pure dream of thought was checked for a moment. A wave of terror came rushing back and she said:

"I thought you didn't want me any more. Back there — after what she said to you."

He could only tell her again that he wanted her more than ever and that now, for the first time, he understood her and all about her and why she had come there. She lifted her face and smiled.

"Dance with me again," she said. "I love to dance with you. That'll be a wonderful day when you can really dance and we can go well together."

He said he was as awkward as a hog in a sack.

"No," she said. "You'll get it — all of a sudden. Like skating. And then you'll see — we'll go round and round again, just like one person."

As they danced again she felt him relaxing. His rather heavy boots kicked up a dry shower of dust. After the second or third dance she felt thirsty. He said he was thirsty too and went away to fetch her some beer.

While she was waiting for him to come back she stood leaning against the tree trunk, staring at the water. Upstream the curve of the bridge was like a black elbow crooked sharp above the river. The current came down under it swift and crosswise. She could actually see an eddy of it, curdling round and round in the reflection of a group of pale green stars.

"That's where I'll go," she thought, "when you don't love me any more."

The thought was with her, quick and solemn, before she was aware of it. Then it floated away, like a fragment of something in the dark stream.

A moment later he was back with two tall glass jugs of beer.

"Big crowd in there tonight," he said. "Well — big for a Saturday. You should see it on Feast Sunday — in July. People come here from twenty or thirty or fifty miles round. Altogether there's fifty Feasts that Sunday. Don't you remember it from last year?"

"I don't remember much — "

"We stood outside and looked at the glow in the sky," he said. "Don't you remember? You thought the town was on fire."

"So I did. I remember."

She did not remember.

"That was Feast Sunday. The first Sunday in July. The day we have green peas and new potatoes for the first time."

"Another month," she said. "If you practiced a bit you could dance quite well by then."

They did not dance much more that evening. They stood for a long time under the chestnut trees, slowly drinking beer. Sometimes he kissed her wet lips or the hollow of her neck or the side of her hair. The sound of fiddles and the piano was pleasant at a distance. The silence between the dances was like a thin singing echo over the water and the dark June fields.

"This is a day I'll never forget," she said. "The water cress and the new dress and what you said to me and now tonight and the dancing."

When the beer was finished he stood in front of her,

holding her with one hand and counting with the other the bars of buttons that were, as Wainwright said, like a bead frame across the front of her dress.

She leaned her head against the trunk of the tree and felt her entire body stir and quiver as he touched her. Finally he held her with both hands and said:

"I love your dress. It's the best dress I've ever seen — "

"It's the best dress I ever had," she said. "I never had a dress like this."

"All you want now is a hat."

"Oh! no. My hat's all right — "

"I'll buy you a hat for Big Feast Sunday," he said. "The right color. To go with the dress."

"Oh! no — you bought me the dress, you bought me too much already."

He began to say that he had seen a hat once that he liked, a hat with a feather in it. "It came across the front like this," he said. With one hand he made a curling movement just below the frontal line of her hair. She felt it brush her tenderly, like a feather. "Then the hat was a bit to one side," he said. "Like that — a little bit down on one eye. That's the sort of hat I'd like you to have."

"You bought me too much already," she said. "Anyway you'd never get a hat like that in this town."

"Where could we get it?"

"I don't need a hat, I really don't need one."

"Where could we get it?"

"I don't know. Bedford perhaps. Perhaps Northampton."

"We'll go to Bedford," he said.

"But that's expensive — all that way — traveling by train!"

He laughed again. With measured tenderness he began counting the buttons on her dress. She felt the light pressure of his fingers on the budlike buttons and then once, centrally, on the points of her breasts.

Suddenly she wanted to cry out that he had given her all and more than she wanted; she had so much more than she deserved. Now, at last, it was her own turn to give. "I'll give you anything," she thought, "everything, anything you want," but she could find no way of saying what she felt and at last she heard him say:

"We could dance in Bedford. You wanted me to practice my dancing."

"And what will your mother think? — a new dress and then dancing and then me in a new hat," she said. "What will she say?"

"We'll go to Bedford," he said.

She pressed her head against the back of the tree, moving it backwards and forwards. She heard the fiddles die in the bar. Silence sang marvelously away again across the river and the fields and she said:

"If you promise it's the last thing you'll give me then I'll come. I'll come if you promise me that."

He laughed. He said he promised. She knew she did not believe it. Then she laughed too and knew that she did not want to believe it. An owl called from a tree up the river and a woman shrieked at a joke in the bar. In a sudden turn of water under the bridge a whole galaxy of stars broke and swam in a whirlpool and were drowned in the black elbow of shadow.

"It's time to go home," he said, "before the owls get you."

In a final surge of joy she took hold of his hands and pressed them against her body, feeling it waking young and eager through the smooth new dress.

"I'm so happy. This is the happiest day of my life," she said.

I X

IT took them most of a Saturday afternoon and the early part of an evening, a month later, to find the hat he wanted.

About five o'clock a burst of thunder rain came up the broad river from the direction of the sea and left the town of Bedford, low in its valley, heavy with damp and sultry air. By six o'clock he had seen her stand before a score of mirrors, shaking his head at hats that were too high for her neat dark head or too low and wide for her delicate ears.

"You're set on that feather, aren't you?" she said. "You won't rest till we get the feather."

With a sort of rooted patience he watched her try another hat. From the upstairs windows of the shop he saw rain pouring from a gold-bronze thunder sky. Inside the shop three heads of Bella in a large rose-bowered hat of blue-green straw were reflected in oval mahogany panels of a milliner's mirror and with them white pouring slants of summer rain.

"How about this one?"

"No," he said. "That isn't you."

An image of perfection had become fixed in his mind. He could not get it out. She went near to exasperation once as he shook his head at a hat of coffee brown, with a feather of the shape he wanted: its curl like a question mark horizontally laid across the front of her hair.

"No," he said, "your hair's too dark for that."

"I'm not perfect, you know," she said sharply. "I can't be perfect. If they haven't got it I shall have to take the next best thing."

He had no intention of taking the next best thing. "We'll get it," he said.

With obstinacy he sat down and waited for another hat.

Presently it was so dark for a few minutes that the milliner's assistant put a match to a gas bracket on the wall behind the mirrors. Between the green of gaslight and the thunder glow of the sky he saw the face of Bella crowned with a hat of peacock green. It had a feather across the front of it almost of the shape he wanted.

Then, outside, the light began paling. The green of the gas mantle gradually looked white. The sky became pure yellow, without rain. Finally as she turned he saw that the hat, no longer bathed in that queer summer thunder light, was not a peacock green. It was much lighter. He thought it was much more like the green of young wheat as it rises to ear.

"That's it. That's the one," he said. There was a certain touch of triumph in his voice. "I knew we'd find it somewhere."

"Well!" She could not resist a temptation to mock him

slightly. She laughed and bowed. "Now we know *one* person will be happy."

"Aren't you happy then?" he said.

"Oh! You know I am! I love it," she said. "I love it if it's what you wanted."

Then the assistant said: "Would you like to wear it or shall I put it in a box for you?"

"Keep it on," he said. "Wear it."

"But it's still raining. It hasn't left off yet — "

"Wear it," he said. "I want you to wear it. We'll buy an umbrella if it rains."

She wore the hat. He took her arm and guided her through the streets of the town. With pride he took her through the market, down to the river bridge and back again. Under wet market stalls there was a smell of ripe strawberries in the air. He said he fancied strawberries to eat; and perhaps a plate of ham. From the window of a teashop they watched the sky finally clear to the pure washed blue of summer after rain. They ate a plate of ham with tea and rolls of bread and butter, and then a plate of strawberries with cream. Then he said he fancied a second plate of strawberries; and she said as she watched him eat them:

"Anyone would think you'd had nothing for a week."

"I feel I can eat now we've got the hat," he said.

Several times he looked up with such affection at the hat that at last she said:

"I'm sorry for that awful thing I said. I could have bitten my tongue out. I didn't mean to mock you."

"What thing?"

"About being happy."

He seemed to have forgotten her remark about being happy. He said simply:

"You look perfect. You look just how I wanted."

He said this in such a way that she felt all her happiness come back. Perhaps now, at last, in the new dress, with the new hat, she was as perfect as he wanted her to be.

"We'll have a boat on the river," he said. "And then a dance and some supper. I think they dance at the Angel. I think I've heard Jedd say so. Then we can catch the last train home."

"I'd love to dance," she said. "I feel like dancing."

The seats of the boat were wet with rain. The boatman wiped them with a towel before putting the velvet cushions back. The air was bright and close after the storm and Con took off his jacket and rolled up his shirt sleeves. She made as if to unpin her hat for fear of losing it on the river but he said:

"No. Keep the hat on. I can look at it while I row."

He rowed placidly under willows, letting the boat glide in long quiet drifts. Several times he looked again with such affection at the hat that she was wonderfully moved with happiness. And once his stare at it was so long and soft in adoration that she said:

"Don't look at me like that. I can't bear it if you look at me like that. Not here, on the river."

It was between nine and ten before they began dancing.

The back upstairs room at the Angel, with its frieze of hunstmen and dado of varnished pine and its piano and pots of palm, reminded her for a moment or two of a room where she had sometimes danced at the Three Bells. It seemed like a lifetime since she had come from the sea. Now she was not, she thought, the same person any longer; she would never again be the same person; she would never again be so fortunate, she thought at that moment, or so happy.

"I must just take my hat and leave it in the cloakroom," she said.

"Must you? Couldn't you dance in it?"

"Now, Con!" she said. "Not in the hat."

The cloakroom was downstairs, at the back end of a central passage that led past a billiard room and through to the street and the bars. She could hear a tick-clock of billiard balls. She caught sight of arcs of green-covered gaslight on tables as she turned at the banisters and went upstairs.

Afterwards she often remembered how little they talked while they were dancing. He was already getting much looser and easier in all the steps; he was already leading her and carrying her away; he had mastered the waltz very well. Most of that evening was a long dusty whirl under a spinning frieze of huntsmen, with Con holding her at arm's length, so that he looked full into her face at the same time.

Once he said: "I'm glad it rained today. Perhaps it's

cleared the air and it won't rain tomorrow now. Feast tomorrow."

"We mustn't forget the train," she said. "We'd look like a pair of stupids if we missed the train."

"Eleven-nineteen," he said. "We got time for just one more."

She let her body unbend a little; he held her a little more closely as they danced for the last time. At the end of it the three violins and the piano were getting ready to play an encore and Con was getting ready to dance again when she said:

"No: don't let's spoil it and have to rush. You go down and get yourself a glass of beer while I find my hat and comb my hair."

"Don't be long," he said. "I'll meet you at the door."

"It was so perfect," she said.

After she had combed her hair and found her hat she came into the passage from the cloakroom with the hat still in her hands. Afterwards she would often wonder what might have happened if she had decided to wear the hat instead; what difference it might have made if she had stayed a moment or two longer, putting it straight and pinning it on.

Instead she came into the passage and past the billiard room without the hat. The passage was crowded. She found herself pushed aside for a moment by people who wanted to go upstairs.

A second later someone was calling her name.

"Bella! Bella! — hey there, Bella. Hey, Bella, hang on a minute there! — "

She turned.

"It's me," he said. "Arch Wilson. It's me. Don't you know me now?"

He stood at the door of the billiard room, half in and half out of it. His cue was still in one hand. In the other he had a lump of blue chalk. He screwed it on the tip of the cue. Its dry squeak on the tip made her blood run cold.

"Well, Bella — young Bella," he said. "I still can't believe it's Bella. How's Bella? You live here?"

"I've got to go now," she said. "Someone's waiting. I've got a train to catch."

"Ah! come on, Bella. Not for a minute."

A high collar lengthened his throat, jerking up his chin as he laughed. The mealy, malty voice was the same. She felt another wave of coldness chilling her spine as he chalked the cue-tip.

"Ah! Bella. You don't look a bit different."

"I don't want to talk to you," she said.

"Where do you live?" he said. "Here? How is it I didn't see you?"

"I live at Nenweald. I'm going to catch a train there — "

"Nenweald, eh?"

"Where you said you lived."

"Bedford. Bedford. That's what I said."

Hatred locked her voice so that for some seconds she could not speak again. She heard him laugh. From behind him, in the billiard room, someone called, "Arch! You playing or not? Come on if you're playing!" and he said, quickly, head down over the billiard cue:

"I got to get back now with the fellows. When do I see you?"

"I don't want to see you. Not now. Not any time."

"Nenweald, eh?" The teeth flashed above the uplifting collar, under the sleek light brown mustache. She saw the incredibly light blue, transparent eyes. "I tell you what, I'll be over there. I come there fishing sometimes. I'll be over there tomorrow. Isn't it the Feast or something to-morrow?"

"No," she said. "No. Don't you ever come there — "

"Where?" he said. The eyes held her. "What time?"

"No time," she said. "Never. Not with you."

Hatred and all she had to say to him kept her there, talking and answering, while she struggled to get away. He laughed again. In a gesture of sleeking nonchalance, eyes fixed on her, he brushed two fingers across the light mustache.

"You'll come," he said. "You know you'll come."

"I'm going now," she said. "Don't you come over there — "

"You'll come," he said. "I'll see you. And wear the hat." He gave a last shrill twist of chalk on cue, making her spine run cold. "I like the hat. I'll look for the hat — "

"You come and God help you," she said. "That's all."

He laughed in the old mealy, smoothing way. "All?" he said. "All?"

In the train, alone in a carriage with Con, she sat for a long time in a pain of frozen terror, not speaking. He said once or twice, "You're quiet," and she managed to say, as she had said several times before, how lovely the day had been, how perfect and how much she had loved it all.

"That's why I'm quiet," she said.

"There's one thing we forgot," he said.

"What was that?" she said. "We had everything — we didn't forget anything."

"Gloves," he said.

She wanted to cry. In that extreme moment, as he spoke of gloves, all the suppuration of her hatred against Arch Wilson broke and flooded her. She felt tears pouring harshly into her eyes as she sat there listening and repeating the single simple word:

"Gloves? Gloves? What would I want with gloves?"

He held her hands, first one and then the other.

"I noticed most of the girls had gloves on," he said, "when they were dancing."

She could not speak; she found it hard not to scream at him.

"Long gloves," he said. "White ones, some of them. Like people wear when they're married."

She could only say in answer, with a laugh, in relief, "You'd better save them for that," and he said:

"That's it. That's what I mean to ask you. Will you? — perhaps when we get harvest over?"

"Oh! God," she said.

She shut her eyes and clung to him. She was aware of nothing except the train bumping on through summer darkness. The echo of it throbbed deeply through her body. "Hold me," she began thinking. "Hold me. Don't let me go any more. Don't let anything happen to me. Marry me before anything can happen to me."

He held her there, under the single bowl of naked orange gas flame, pressing his mouth against her hair, speaking once more of the loveliness of the hat, until some time after the train had stopped and the porter had come with his swinging lamp and his shout along the platform:

"All change! All change! All change here! All change!"

She could not sleep. She lay in humid summer darkness and stared for hour after hour at a sky that burned above the town, until after two o'clock, with the rosy glow of the fair. She could hear the big Italian mechanical organs on the steam roundabouts thumping and whining their tunes. Broken now and then by a wild hot whistle of steam, they went round and round and on and on like a nightmare.

At first her thoughts fell into the same simple repeated pattern as the tunes the organs played. In the morning, she thought, she had nothing more to do than say, "You remember Arch Wilson? I saw him yesterday. In Bedford. He spoke to me. He said he was coming here" — that was simple enough to do, easy enough to say.

It seemed another matter to indicate her fear; it was altogether different when she came to express her hatred and revulsion. "I've got Con now," she thought. "I've no need to be afraid. He asked me to marry him. I belong to him." That too was simple enough to say. It was only when she thought more and more of Con himself that her fears began to develop fears and then grow more painful and more complicated.

She began to remember the evening at the Wharf, more than a year before, when she had made the mistake of thinking Arch Wilson was sitting there under the open window of the bar. She remembered the wild rush of Con up the slope between the chestnut trees; the dangling, trembling straw hat, the way the watch had spewed itself from his waistcoat pocket, the way it had danced like a fish on the chain. "I ain't Wilson — Don't break my watch — Bella who?" — it had been an easy mistake to make in a half-light where faces were vague and dresses still had color.

Then she remembered something else. She remembered what she said in answer to the terrified pleading of the straw hat: "I ain't nobody you know, am I? God's truth, I ain't, am I?" And then she remembered not only what she had said — "No, but you could have been" — but why she had said it. She had said it because the search for Wilson was still not over.

But now it was over; all that was finished now. "Some day I'll find you and I'll kill you," she had thought. But now that was over and it seemed like an awful and terrible thing to say. It was wrong to think like that; it was wrong too to make a mistake and let someone suffer the consequences.

"I'll never make a mistake like that again," she thought. "I love you too much — I'll never drag you into that again. I love you too much for that."

Then she remembered the raging scythe in the harvest field; that too had been because of her. Nothing like that, she thought, was ever going to happen again. No mistake, no rage, no fighting — she wanted, now, only the man who had set his heart on a hat with a feather in it, a green dress and a pair of gloves, who loved to dance with her and who looked at her sometimes with such entrancement that in sheer happiness her body ached and melted.

"That's the sort of person you must have been when you hunted butterflies," she thought. "The long days you used to spend in the meadows."

It was nearly three o'clock before she remembered the butterflies and it seemed like a solution to all her complicated thought.

"That's what we could do," she thought. "Take a boat and spend the day on the river. Along the backwater. Out of the way. Where nobody will see us. Arch Wilson nor nobody. All alone."

By that time the music of the Italian organs had stopped on the fairground. A glow of light that seemed to have settled like rose-yellow mist on the lower edges of sky became the first touch of daylight, already breaking.

She was not troubled any longer.

"You can catch butterflies and tell me the names of them," she thought. "Like you always said you would. Catch them without killing them, then show them to me and let them fly away."

It was afternoon, that day, the first Sunday in July, before they could take a boat and row themselves, as she wanted, up into the backwaters of the river.

That Sunday, in the Wainwright household, was a tradition that could not be broken; the day of Fifty Feasts was second only to Christmas Day. The little house was hot with roasting and Wainwright moved about it with starched and avuncular dignity, proud of an altar of three fowls, a sirloin, a large pudding and the first dishes of green peas and new potatoes. He wore a fresh white shoemaker's apron so that the gravy would not splash him as he carved and said, "Let 'em all come!" and wished that Matty and the corporal were there. It did not seem the same, he said, without Matty and the corporal. He wished there were someone to say to him, "Draw the rations, sergeant, and sound the cook-house door!"

Bella sat through this dinner with an assured and growing happiness. The table was crowded with the faces of relatives she had never seen before; men with swag watchchains and thick brown squeaking boots, women whose hats were piled in bedrooms like crowns of flower.

Wainwright identified these relatives for her with expanding pride: "Albert and his wife. Till and Hoppy and their two from Deene. Tom Waters who keeps the Fox at Shelton. Liz and Annie and Ezra from Bourne End. Floss and her husband and Joe from Bletsoe," until he was sure that she knew them all.

"Five thousand people on the market hill last night," he said. "Ten thousand I shouldn't wonder."

"Stretch it, stretch it," Mrs. Wainwright said and Bella was aware of a sense of crowds on all sides, through fifty towns across the midsummer countryside, keeping her secure.

Then towards the end of the meal she was aware of Con nervously stabbing with a spoon at the cloth in front of him. She heard his mother say, "Ah! make a hole big enough to get your fist through, I would," and then with blind gravity he was staring straight in front of him.

"This seems as good a time as any to say it. Bella and me are going to get married. After harvest," he said.

"Hair and teeth!" Wainwright said. "Now *that's* talking! *That's* a thing we got to get the corporal home for!"

She sat quiet, staring before her at a plate on which there were a few yellow crumbs of pastry. An overwhelming impression of staring at another plate, of hearing someone say, "Don't you want your bread? I'll eat it if you don't want it" came rushing back to her. Everyone by that time was talking and laughing at once and above the noise of it she heard Wainwright say:

"Here! Here! That won't do. She's piping her eye!"

"Ah! blab it out," Mrs. Wainwright said. "You got about as much tack as a sow a-layin' on a dillin'."

Everyone laughed at that. She felt herself laughing too, the table swimming before her in a pool of tears.

"And we hope," they all said, "you'll be very happy."

The meadows were still uncleared of hay when she and Con rowed downstream that afternoon and the air was thick with the scent of it. Lying in the boat, sleepy, she heard a kingfisher travel past with a thin high scream that was like the long fading scratch of a pencil on a slate. The sun was hot on her face as she lay flat on the cushions and presently Con leaned forward and covered her face with a big clean handkerchief.

"You'll get sick, lying there in the sun."

"I'm asleep already," she said.

Some time later he said, "Man a-fishing," and through her thick sleepiness she heard him call:

"Any luck?"

"Not a touch."

"Too bright, I expect," Con said. "Too hot. They'll bite about seven. What are you using?"

"Maggots."

"Sometimes they'll go for a caddis when it's hot," Con said.

She felt the shadow of a bridge slide over her face, then the hot cut of sun again as the boat cleared it on the other side.

"I thought at first he had a funny sort of float," Con said. "Red with a blue top on. Then I saw it was a blue dragonfly sitting there."

"Did you?" she said.

Her voice was very drowsy; he said he could see her breath puffing the handkerchief. The kingfisher scratched the surface of the afternoon again in a long high squeak. Some time later she felt the boat cutting through reeds. It was cooler and the shade above her was moving with the turn and whisper of poplar leaves.

"Where are we?"

"In the back-brook. The same place we were that night we started dancing."

She did not answer; he said again, teasing, that she was asleep and she said:

"Nearly now. Too much dinner."

"Always the same on Feast Sunday," he said. "We might starve all winter long but the Feast is different. Everybody eats till they bust on Feast Sunday."

She heard him tying up the boat. A deep wave of warm air, all hay scent, ran evenly up the backwater and settled itself like a bird brooding between the banks of reed and rose. For ten minutes or so she actually went to sleep, unaware of him moving up and down the grass slope between the poplars, and then she was awake again, wondering where she was.

She sat up in the boat and saw him lying halfway up the bank, one hand cupped above a head of ragwort. She remembered the butterflies. She saw his hand close over the ragwort flower with the neat smoothness of the back of a watch. A moment later she jumped from the boat and called:

"What did you get? What sort?"

"Cinnabar," he said. "Come and see it. Some folks call it a pink underwing."

Black and cinnabar-red the moth broke from his fingers as he opened them. In release it flew up and down for some seconds on the same trembling vertical line. "Like a ball at a shooting gallery," he said. "It's a common sort. I used to catch them by the thousand. I love that red though, and the black. You'd look nice in a dress like that."

"Oh! you and your dresses. Be satisfied."

"What with?"

"Me," she said. "Aren't I enough for you? You couldn't keep it, could you? You had to tell them."

"Like I was when I was a boy." He grinned. "I'd catch a red admiral or a hawk down here and run all the way home with it because I couldn't wait."

A crowd of common blues, like smoke, broke from the grasses. Farther up the bank the air was full of burnets, brown-gold on heads of clover, and small fritillaries bouncing and poising on bushes of blackberry. He grabbed a bee from a spray of dewberry flower.

"You'll get stung! You'll get stung," she said. "I wonder how you dare!" and he laughed and said:

"This is the sort we call grabbers. They've got orange behinds and yellow heads. They don't sting. Grab one!"

"Me? — and get stung?"

"They don't sting," he said. "Look! — orange and yellow." He cupped his hand against her ear and she heard the grumbling terror of bee wings beating imprisoned in

the palm of his hand. "It's easy. Yellow head, orange behind. They can't hurt you."

"Not me." She laughed and shuddered. "Not me. I
wouldn't dare."

The top of the bank was crowned with bushes of hawthorn and alder. For another hour they lay in the thick
shade of them. They talked of marrying and fixed the
wedding for the first Sunday in September. With the far
smell of hay she felt an edge of sweetness that might have
been honeysuckle. It hung on the air with a delicacy she
could not define and she said:

"What shall I wear? What would you like me to wear
that day? Not white — I wouldn't want to wear white.
You know that, don't you?"

"I like colors best," he said.

"I could have worn the green," she said. "It would have
saved buying another. But people would say it was un-
lucky. They always do."

"Not the green," he said. "You know what I had in
mind?"

"What?"

"Yellow. There's a butterfly called a clouded yellow. A
sort of half-and-half yellow. That's what I fancied."

She could only say, with simplicity, with quiet deep
gladness:

"Whatever it is I shall like it. I know I will if you want
it. That's all I care."

She remembered the rest of the afternoon as a dream
of small brown and blue and crimson moths sparking and

smoking from seeds of grasses and flowers of thistle and clover as the two of them walked up and down the low bank in the sun. Across the valley the heat quivered in whiteness, setting haycocks floating and trembling like pale brown corks. Bells started to ring from across the meadows and he said, "Must be nearly six. We ought to be getting back," and she said, "Why? What have we got to get back for? Let's stay until it's dark now."

She was aware again of wanting to hide herself; she wanted to lie safely in grasses, under the poplars, away from the crowd.

"Till dark?" he said. "And miss Feast supper? My father would never forgive you. My mother would never speak to you again — "

"All over a thing like that?" she said. "All over a supper? I ate so much at dinnertime — "

"Ah! but this's a day," he said. "You forget there's only one day like this in a year."

She lay down in the grasses again and begged him to stay a little longer. She folded him down to her, laughing at him, exciting him with little turns of her face and then by putting a grass in her mouth as he tried to kiss her. The stalk of grass was like a tassel of feather brushing his face as she moved it to and fro with her lips. She saw a darker start of blue in the fair blue eyes, a touch of impatience with her, the first for a long time, and he said:

"Stop it! You want to make me mad?"

"I'll stop it if you'll stay a little longer," she said. "Come and lie down with me and stay another hour." She let the grass fall from her mouth. A little golden pollen from it, like dust, dropped from the dancing head of flower. She licked it away with her wet tongue, laughing: "Come on. Don't look like that. I love you. I won't do it any longer."

Because of this it was nearly eight o'clock before they began to row back upstream. As they moved away a crowd of dragonflies burst from the reeds with a sound like dry tissue blowing away. All the heat and dreaminess and quietness of the afternoon seemed to break with them and she said:

"That was lovely. We have some lovely days."

As he shipped oars to go under the first bridge he turned his head and said:

"Wonder if the fellow's still fishing. He was by that doddle-willow," and some moments later she heard him calling:

"Any luck?"

A second later she sat rigid in the stem of the boat. A dragonfly broke like an electric spark from the tip of scarlet float as the rod twitched and a voice called:

"Hey, Bella! Out on the *Skylark?* I told you I'd see you, didn't I?"

A blankness of terror hit her like a chill of fog. The bank where Arch Wilson sat on a campstool vanished out of sight. A great undertow of bright green weed went swimming past the boat, shot with sun, and she felt as if she drowned away in it, dragged down.

"Who's that? Who is it? I never saw him before."

"Nobody. Nobody."

"Nice day, Bella. Nice for a row. Ah! come on, Bella." The low mealy voice was thick across the water. "Don't say you don't know me."

"Who are you?" Con called.

"Ah! she knows. Ask Bella. Ask her, mister. She knows."

"Take no notice. Take no notice," she said.

She saw Con pressing on the oars. The blades were cutting back through water, checking the boat. She heard another laugh from under the willow tree, a laugh with a twist in it:

"Too fancy for old friends now. Too fancy, eh? Is that it? Too fancy."

"What's your name?" Con said.

"Ah! — ask her, ask Bella. What's it to you?"

"I can damn soon show you."

"Let's go," she said. "Let's go. Let's go home."

"Oh! let's go home!" Wilson mouthed. "Oh! let's go home! Let's go home before Arch Wilson gets me!"

She remembered nothing else for a moment or two but the sickening arc of the boat, too sharp and too fast against the current, as Con pulled it round on a single oar. Then she was aware of the boat nose cutting into fishing line, the crack of it on the rod tip, and Arch Wilson yelling:

"Mind what the hell you're up to! Mind what you're doing, you clumsy sod!"

The boat hit the bank. A twist of line went clean underneath it. The spool of the reel chattered as it pulled. The boat swung parallel to the bank and hit it through a snap of reeds. Her fog of terror lifted. In awful brightness she saw Con leap to the bank and crack his foot on the rod and then rush forward at Wilson.

"Hey, mind my rod. That's a new rod. That's new — "

Wilson picked up the stool. It suddenly collapsed. She heard him shout as he pinched his fingers. The pain seemed to anger him and he swung the stool at Con, who put up his arm. The blow caught him partly on the arm, partly on the back of the head, and he yelled.

A moment later he hit Wilson in the mouth. Wilson fell backwards. His body struck with a queer crackling squeak against his fishing basket. His mouth opened with a look of unprepared fright and a tin of maggots spilled on the bare dry earth about the bole of the tree.

"I'll give you yell at her! I'll give you summat to yell for next time!"

Wilson was staggering about the bank. He was still holding the campstool. Now he swung it over his head, using the force of both hands.

She saw Con swerve and slip backwards and grab an oar. The stool struck his shoulder. Wilson lurched and slipped as he swung the stool and Con hit him full with the oar blade in the nape of the neck. He fell forward on his hands and knees and then tried to get up. Then he fell again and turned over.

She tried to jump from the boat. As Con swung the oar again she was weeping and shouting at the same time:

"You'll kill him! You'll kill him. Oh! my God, what are you doing?"

She saw Wilson's face upturned on the bank. The mustache stood stiffly on the lip, a paintbrush dipped in red. Then the flat blade of the oar came down on it, hitting the eyes. Wilson did not move after the second or third time it struck him.

Her feet tangled themselves in the line. The reel rolled down the bank into water. There was suddenly nothing she could see but Arch Wilson's face bloody where it had rolled into a mass of buttercups, and a spilled heap of maggots writhing white and cleansed in the sun.

Less than a minute later her thoughts became extraordinarily calm and clear.

"He's stopped breathing," she said.

Con was still standing with the oar in his hands; there was a crack in the blade of it and what looked like a tuft of blood in the crack.

"Dead?" he said. "Not dead, is he?" His face was deathly.

She had been bending over Wilson, feeling his wrists and his body under the shirt. She knew that Wilson was dead.

Her thoughts took a sudden leap forward. She got up. She was not aware of being afraid and she said:

"Get into the boat. How much money have you got?"

"Money?" His hands began to jump in huge stiff shudders. She picked up the oar. She saw his hands stabbing into his pockets, unable to hold themselves still. The kingfisher went past, cutting downriver with the long whistle that was again like the scratch of lead on slate and she said:

"Get into the boat. I'll row."

"I've got a sovereign. A sovereign and a few coppers," he said.

"Get in."

He shuddered blindly about the bank. She put out her hands and held him for a moment or two, pressing him to her with strength and calmness, trying to hold him still.

"I've got you," she said. "Hold still if you can."

"What have I done? My God — "

"Hold still now. Never mind about that. I'm with you. I'm going to be with you."

She kissed the side of his face quickly and he got into the boat. His skin was rough with chill and she heard his teeth begin to chatter.

"Lie down on the cushions a little while," she said. "I'll row. I can row."

He lay crumpled in the bottom of the boat, his mouth open. He managed to say something and his words were stuttered out from half-locked jaws.

"Where are we going? What are you going to do?"

"Where's the first lock?" she said.

"About three miles down."

"Near Conygers? Is that it?"

"That's it," he said. "Near the green lane."

She shipped oars under the bridge. Sun and then shade and then sun cut across her face with dazzling triple effect of light and shadow and light.

[199]

"How far does the green lane go?"

"Miles. Out by Saxton and Hargrave and Slapton Springs."

"Slapton Springs." Her mind leaped back, cool and quick. "That's where I went one day with Jedd."

The boat went past the place where the back-brook came in and joined, from under the arch of poplars, the main course of the river. In a trembling rush of sound a breath of wind broke from high leaves. She remembered in that moment all the dream of the afternoon: the cinnabar moth, the blues and browns smoking and sparking from dusty grasses, the scent of honeysuckle, the bees that could be grabbed and did not sting.

For the first time, then or afterwards, her courage broke. She gasped at the air with a sob she could not hold. All the joy of the day, the high crowning movement of evening falling across meadows to the sound of bells, slipped past her with a brittle repetition of the wings of dragonflies rising in gauzy clouds from a mass of reeds. She knew that it would never come back. Nothing like it could ever happen again. The sob choked in her throat. Then she bit her lips, fighting to keep calm, thinking:

"Perhaps I'll never have that again. I can't. But I'll keep you for a while. For a day. Perhaps two. Perhaps a week" — the words Mrs. Wainwright so often used came back and gave her now a curious sense of justification — "if we live and have good luck."

A moment later the mouth of the back-brook disappeared behind a bend of the stream. On the bank opposite the towpath, the bank that fishermen used, willow herb grew in high lush pink walls. She rowed so close to it that she sometimes tipped the stalks with the blade of the oar.

A water rat came out of this wall of flower and looked at her and dived. It struck her then that this was the only living creature they had seen. Her calmness and courage came back. "We'll have the luck," she thought. "Nobody has seen us. We'll have the luck."

"Isn't there another bit of a back-brook just before the lane?" she said.

"That's the old cut."

He was still lying in the bottom of the boat, trying to calm the violent shudders of his hands by locking them under his armpits, like a man pained with cold.

"The old cut round to Pidgeons Mill. Afore they pulled it down."

"I know. We can leave the boat there."

The back cut was so choked with reed and willow herb and waterweed and the pads of waterlily that she had to paddle the boat for the last half mile to where the mill had been. The cut had been built to avoid the lock. Nothing came along it now that the mill was down.

A square cake of stones remained where the mill had stood. A narrow bridge between the old mill doors and the opposite bank made a tunnel of ten yards or so where the water funneled into the millrace beyond. She heard a sluice pouring away with a hiss beyond the bridge. It was not quite twilight and she wondered what time it was. Then she saw the tunnel and said:

"Help me pull into the bank. We'll leave it here."

Two minutes later she let the boat glide out of her hands. Then with an oar she guided and pushed it down the tunnel. She heard it strike the iron of the sluice gate at the other end. She let the oar float after it.

Then she stood up and brushed the lapels of his jacket and smoothed them with her hands. He was still shaking. His forehead was a honeycomb of sweat beads under tangled hair.

"Give me your handkerchief. Let me wipe your forehead. Have you got a comb? Comb your hair a bit straight with your hands."

As his hands touched the back of his head she saw him wince. She turned him round and saw a gash in his head, a matting of bloody hair above the nape, and she said:

"How did you get that? When did that happen?"

"That was when he hit me with the stool."

"Did he hit you first with the stool?"

He swayed from one foot to another, touching his face with one hand, trying to remember.

"Try to think if he hit you first with the stool."

"I can't think."

"I think he did," she said. "I seem to remember it." She began to speak with a concentration that was compressed and fanatical. "I can't remember it clear enough now, but I shall remember. I'll think. I'll think till I do remember."

As they began to walk away the air was so still that she heard a clock begin to chime its quarters in the direction of the town.

She held him by the sleeve as she listened. She counted the quarters, three of them, and then the hour. The strokes of the clock seemed to hang for a few seconds high above the valley after the last had died.

"Nine," she said. "Can you walk? Hold on to me."

The lane was a green bank between double high hedgerows that went diagonally out of the valley through fields, almost due east, crossing hard roads at right angles. She remembered afterwards mile after mile of sloes green on old high bushes of blackthorn and trees of elderberry half in green fruit, half in flower. In places the bushes had grown across the track and into each other, leaving a path only wide enough for a sheep between.

They did not talk much, but sometimes she asked him questions about distances. How far did the track go? Did he remember? How far was it to Slapton Springs?

She thought for some time of a railway. A line went up the valley, following the river, and forty miles away a number of other lines fed out to the north, the east and the fenlands. Then she rejected the railway. It was not only too risky but she thought:

"I walked here. If I did that by myself, how I was then, we can do it together."

She began to think more and more of the sea. It was perhaps eighty or ninety miles to the sea. "We could walk at night," she thought. As her thoughts began to turn to the sea they cleared still further. She remembered one by one the faces of several seafaring men who brought small colliers and boats loaded with ballast and lime and timber up to the jetties by the Three Bells and then afterwards sailed upriver to pick up wheat and barley.

She remembered a man named Luther Rogers who, whenever he saw her, had a curious greeting:

"I'd like to fix you to my old tub for a figurehead. There's nobody like you for putting a smile in the beer."

He was a fattish, easy-eyed, loose-mouthed man who spoke with an occasional inconsistent stutter. She remembered his way of wearing his seafaring cap jammed down on one ear. Because of that you could never tell if he wore one gold ear-ring or a pair.

"Every time I come across from the Hook you know what I start thinking about? A good drop o' beer with a smile in it. I get sick o' that Dutchy stuff. It's got as much kick in it as dandelion drink."

Just before darkness fell she saw, at a place where the track crossed a road, the lights of a house.

"I think that's a pub," Con said. The walk had calmed him a little; now she felt him begin to tremble again. "You better go and look and see if the road's all clear."

"If it's a pub we're going to stop," she said. "We'll want food. We can't go on without food."

"Not in there," he said. "Not inside. I couldn't face that."

"I'll go in," she said. "I'll get some bread and cheese and a glass of bitter and bring it out to you."

She felt his hands quivering, hot now, in the growing darkness.

"Don't tremble like that," she said.

"What have I gone and done?" he said. "My God — killing somebody — what have I done?"

"Don't think about it." She held him with great calmness. She kissed his face once or twice and touched his hand with one hand. "Come on now — you'll be better after a drink. You need a drink. We've got a long way to go."

Just before she left him sitting on the bench along the wall outside the pub and went into the bar she had another brief recollection of Rogers:

"If I ever git another tub, which ain't very likely, I be damned if I don't call her *Bella*. That's a decent name for a ship. And remember — anything you want, any time."

The little bar, with its varnished doors and counter, was almost empty. The landlord, in his shirt sleeves, cut two thick wedge triangles of cheese and drew two mugs of beer and she said, as she paid for them:

"It's hot. I'll take it outside."

"It is hot, that. Quiet an' all. Everybody down at the Feast today. You bin down there?"

"No," she said. "I'm not one for crowds."

The single oil lamp hanging from the low ceiling was hardly bright enough to do more than put a touch of honey on the foam of the beer; but when she went back into the bar to take the glasses he leaned over the counter and peered in the light of it and touched her shoulder.

"Turn round." She felt her heart give a great start of terror; she stood rigid against a wave of sickness. "You got tuthri burrs on the back o' your dress. I noticed them fust time, when you went out the door."

She heard him laugh; she felt the queer dry grip of thistle burrs as he pulled them one by one from the stuff of her dress.

"Time o' the year to git burrs on you. Layin' about in fields." He laughed moistly, in a series of dribbles. "Eh? Stick to you like sweethearts."

She gave a short quiet laugh too. Then her calm and confidence came back.

After that they walked on for nearly another hour. They had drunk the beer but she had wrapped the bread and cheese in his handkerchief and now she carried it in her hands. The light of July stars was bright enough for her to see a haystack some way before they got to it but it was not until they had been lying beside it for some time that she said:

"This is new hay. This stack isn't finished. Somebody'll be making an early start here in the morning."

They got up and walked on and then lay down again, a quarter of a mile away, in a wood of hazels. He took off his coat and they drew it over themselves.

"Have a sleep. Try to sleep," she said.

In a windless night the air was quiet and heavy with the scent of hay. After some time she heard him gulping with great sobs in the darkness, his nerve broken, and she comforted him for a long time without saying anything, holding his body hard against her own.

"Tomorrow I'm going to think all through it. Every bit of it," she said finally. "How it happened."

"What are you going to do?" he said. "They'll be after us tomorrow — "

She thought again of the sea; but all she said was:

"The man in the bar, at the pub, he was funny. He found some thistle burrs on my dress. He said it was the time of the year to get burrs on you, lying in fields. He said they stuck to you like sweethearts."

Soon after that he was asleep, exhausted. For a long time she did not sleep. She lay watching a planet, big, bright green, appear and disappear like a swinging lantern as it went down to the west beyond the mass of summer branches.

"You won't take him," she thought. "You won't get him from me."

Later she fell asleep too and was waked by the sound of haymakers coming up the lane. There were seven of them, four men and three women; she heard the dancing jangle of hayfork tines on the floor of the wagon as it went bumping past on the dried clay ruts to the field. One of the women was quite old and was wearing an old-fashioned sprigged bonnet with strings. A man was riding side-back on the nearer of the two horses. Two big yellow feed bags were slung over the collar, which were crowned with two curled brass scrolls, and the man held one of the brasses with his right hand. In his left he was holding a piece of bread, gnawing it and gulping it down. He stared across the fields and into the wood with dazed morning eyes and did not see her.

She woke Con and they began walking. The bloom on the many young green sloes was almost pure white with summer dew. The lane began to go uphill. At the crest of the rise they stopped and looked down at the country beyond and she said:

"Where are we? How far have we come now?"

His eyes hung painfully on morning distances. A twist in his neck from the blow at the back gave him a hunched appearance that worried her.

"That looks like Staughton church," he said.

"How far have we come then?"

"Nine mile or more. About that."

She was disappointed; the long green lane had seemed much farther. She saw him give several pained half-paralyzed turns of his neck and she said:

"How is your head? Does it hurt still?"

"It aches a bit. I can't get it round."

"In a little while we'll stop," she said. "We'll find a brook somewhere and I'll bathe it."

As they walked on her mind, sharpened by sleep and morning, began to go through the events of the previous afternoon and carefully separate them like a comb. She saw the swing of the campstool as Arch Wilson lifted it. She saw the turn of Con's head as he moved to duck the blow. Over and over again she thought:

"If he hadn't moved like that it would have hit him in the face. Perhaps on the temple. Then he would have been killed."

Half an hour later they sat by a brook. Water cress in

high summer flower choked the passage of water where it came down through willows and banks of reed. A slime of iron reddened the water line and made him say:

"I fancy this is the brook that comes down from Slapton Springs. It goes into the river near the old North-Western Station."

They ate some of the bread and cheese and she bathed the gash in his head. Under the matted hair, after she had washed it, the bone was blue, the cut about two inches long and jagged. He accepted the pain of it dully. It hardly seemed important enough to matter.

But she said: "Try to remember. Did he hit you first?"

"I can't remember. I remember him yauping at me, yauping about you. And then I was on the bank."

"Keep thinking over it," she said. "Try and see if you can see it again in your mind."

"I can't think," he said. "It's black when I start thinking."

"We'll have a drink of water and a wash before we go on," she said. "Wash your face now and you'll feel better."

He took off his jacket and knelt down and washed his face and hands. As he got up off his knees he turned and saw that she had taken off her dress. Her petticoat was white, with short sleeves in it. Her arms were plumper than they had ever been. The flesh of them had small smooth pores that gave it the tight texture of apple skin and he saw it shining sallow and soft in the morning sun.

She turned, saying "I wish I had a comb," and then she

saw him standing there, arrested, staring at her, eyes loving and pained. For the first time she gave a little laugh.
His face was still wet from the water of the brook. His arrested confusion woke all her tenderness.

"What's the matter?" she said. "You look as if you've
never seen a girl without her dress before."

"I never did," he said. "Except Nell."

She began to say something about taking off her top
petticoat and carrying it and keeping it clean so that she
had a change, but she did not finish all she had to say.

"We were going to be married. We were going to be
married," she heard him say, "but now —" She knew
what he was thinking. "Oh! my Christ," he whispered.

His terror had the effect of bringing back, once again,
her calmness and courage. She spoke in practical terms of
her petticoat, his jacket and waistcoat. She said they could
fold them up and make a bundle of them so that they
would be fresh for them, a change, later.

"Perhaps I could go into a shop somewhere and buy a
little handbag to put them in. In case it rains. You'll need
a razor too."

"You can't go into places. They'll be looking for us all
over the show —"

"Perhaps if I go in soon it'll be all right," she said.
"Perhaps they won't have found him yet. He came from
Bedford. He didn't have a boat. It might be late today
before they missed him."

His horror at the recollection of Arch Wilson lying
bloodily among a mass of high-drawn buttercups was too

much for him as he stood there staring at her, fresh and
naked-armed in the morning sun. He rocked his face in
his hands, whispering terribly again:

"Oh! my Christ, my Christ Almighty," and then asked
her once again where they were going and what they were
going to do.

And again, calmly, she said:

"We'll make for the sea. We'll get there. I walked this
way by myself and I had trouble then. The two of us can
walk back again."

It was about three o'clock in the afternoon when they
came to a rise of ground, a big sweep of isolated pasture
above parklike fields of cedar and beech and lime, that
she thought looked in a strange way familiar and friendly.
An hour and a half before that she had left him lying in a
wood while she walked a quarter of a mile or so to a vil-
lage whose squat spire stuck up like a flint head from
among a ring of chestnut trees. She had bought a razor,
a stick of soap and shaving brush for him, a loaf and some
cheese and a small cheap straw dress basket to put them
in. She had bought a morning newspaper. There was
nothing in it of either Arch Wilson or themselves and she
said:

"Nobody seemed to take much notice. That's why I
waited till after dinner. They're sleepier then."

A hollow of parkland opened out below her. A house
with lids of red-and-white sunblinds at the windows lay
in the center of it, under a sky of broken high white
cloud.

She stopped to stare at it for a moment or two and then remembered.

"I came by here once with Jedd," she said. "We stopped and looked at that house. That day before he went back from furlough."

They walked on and she said:

"I remember what I said that day. I said I couldn't have been happier if I lived in a big house like that. That was how I felt yesterday."

A moment later, before he could say anything, something made her turn her head and look the other way. A road that circled the parkland doubled round the hollow in a long sweep that lost itself in a stretch of willow trees. In a breath of wind she saw the leaves of the willows turn gray-white in the sun. A break in the mass of leaves showed a roof like a rain-darkened haystack and she said:

"I know that house too. It's where a man and his wife make baskets. Jedd used to go there with his father. Did you ever go?"

She turned to look at him. His face was gray with fatigue. The lids of the eyes were pouched and wrinkled at the edges, the pupils dark blue between.

"What house?"

"Jedd said you could get tea there. Your father said they had the best water cress in the world."

"Where?" he said. "Where? I never went there."

She was suddenly scared by his look of distracted tiredness; she saw his head give the strangest disjointed sort of rock.

"Come on," she said. "We'll have a rest there. We'll have a cup of tea."

They walked to the house. A woman who had been picking red currants from bushes veiled with old lace curtains came through a small triangular patch of potatoes and rows of podding peas on hazel sticks. The house was a hundred and fifty yards from the road. Behind it the plantations of osier were thick, gold-barked and pale sage-green, on a dark stretch of marshy land.

"Well, we gin it up tuthri summers back. The teas," the woman said. "Time as Sherwood fell and twisted his back. Wasn't a great lot in it anyway."

She wiped her red currant-stained fingers on the corners of her apron. Her face was broad and easy-eyed, with a grayish mustache thick on a quivering upper lip.

"Still, I can get y' a cup. Dessay I might have a few cresses too. Y' ain't of 'urry are you?"

"No," Bella said. "Not for an hour or so."

"Sit yourselves down inside then. It's cooler there."

By the side door of the house, under a hovel thatched with a foot-thick pile of osier peelings, a small man in a black cap and moleskins sat weaving a basket.

"See for a mite o' cress, Arth," the woman said. "Young couple here a-dyin' fer a cup o' tea."

"I be dalled," the man said. "Ain't had nobody drop in since I got back from th' infirmary. Don't see nobody much up here, one week's end to another."

He moved off with a gait that twisted the right hip in a winding, arching turn and the woman said:

H. E. BATES

"Slipped on a wet bank and hit hisself on osier stump. All done of a minute. Twelve months in Bedford infirmary — so long we had to shut the house down. Went to live with my sister there."

She seemed glad to talk; she came in and out of a small parlor a dozen times to lay a cloth, to bring cups and saucers, to alter the set of the blinds against the sun, and finally to bring tea and bread-and-butter and currant jelly and cresses.

"Dessay you'll find the jelly a bit on the sweet side. I fancy I got it a bit on the sweet side last year. You want a mite o' salt with your cresses?"

In the yellow light made by the partly lowered blinds Bella watched Con several times bring the cup to his face, hold it there and then put it down without drinking. A horsehair sofa with an antimacassar in wool of blue and rose and magenta-purple stood under the window. After the first sip of tea he got up and groped slowly towards it.

"I think I'll lay down for a bit."

A moment later he was feeling his way blindly out into sun. She heard him being terribly sick on the path outside. After some moments he came back and lay down, face turned away from her, shuddering.

"Ain't well?" the woman said. "I was just off back to finish the currants when I heard him. Fetching his heart up."

"A touch of the sun," she said.

[214]

"Well, he can rest here," the woman said. "Rest as long as he likes. Are you going far?"

She said quickly:

"As far as St. Neots. We thought we'd get the carrier from Kimbolton — "

"Carrier don't run now. And the trains are just about as orkard as they know how to be. You don't get nowhere up here 'ithout you walk it. Anythink I can do?"

"He'll be all right," she said. "It's just a rest he needs."

After the woman had gone back to the currants Bella knelt down by the sofa. She held his cold-roughened hands in her own. In the gray face the eyes had sunk a shade lower under puffed, creased lids. The lips were pulled sideways like elastic overstretched and ready to snap.

"We'd better get on," he said. "Better get out of here — "

"I think we could stay here," she said. "I mean for the night. If I asked her."

He did not answer.

"Shall I ask her? It would be all right. You heard what they said — nobody ever comes up here. No carrier's cart or anything. It would be all right."

Sickness and horror had beaten him into a state where she did not need to wait for any answer.

"I'll ask her," she said.

She walked out into the sun, across the potato patch and into a clump of currant trees beyond. The afternoon was full of surging summer quietness, without a breath of air between the osiers, the house and the spinney of young ash that cut off the road.

"Have to go through one bedroom to git to another, though, that's th' only thing," the woman said. "You're welcome if you don't mind that. That suit you?"

All the scent of summer was thick and warm in the little garden, among blood-bright berries, peas climbing their hazel sticks and purple potato flowers.

"Yes, that will suit us," she said.

"I'll tell you what wouldn't hurt him," the woman said, "if he's sick. A little camomile tea. Git him to have a lay-down for an hour and I'll bring him a cup."

He took off his shoes and jacket and lay down in a small whitewashed room on the sunny side of the house. The tea refreshed him. The bed was pretty with a white frilled valance that touched a floor covered with bit-rugs in paisley patterns of red and brown.

Her feet were tired after walking and for some time she sat in the same room, bathing them in a big flowered washbasin by the window. She looked out of the window and said:

"There's rows and rows of raspberries. And plum trees. And beans. The woman's feeding hens." She reached to the washstand for her comb and began combing out her hair. The feeling of combing her hair and bathing her feet at the same time filled her with restfulness. It even seemed, after a time, as if nothing had happened: that Arch Wilson, the boat, the fight and the walking by night and through the day had never happened. She was un-afraid again and she said:

"This is the sort of place I'd have liked to stay in for our honeymoon. Where you couldn't see anybody and you could stay in bed all day."

The thought stuck in her mind. The evening was calm with a breathlessness in which even the leaves of the willows hardly turned. For supper they ate part of a cold leveret with cold new potatoes on which dark leaves of mint were still printed. The raspberries had cream on them and there were cups of milk to drink.

"I count he's feeling better," the woman said. "Tell that be the way he's eating. They allus say the air's good here. They say you start eating like a thacker here."

"Never want to move," Sherwood said. "Never want to go nowheer. We got the cow and a couple o' stores and a sow all the time and vittles and fruit a-new in the garden. What sense is there going anywheer?"

"You want egg fer your breakfast?" his wife said. "You needn't git up. I'll bring it up to you."

"Two and half acres altogether," Sherwood said. "Near enough. A-wintertime I'm a-cutting osiers and summer-time I'm a-basketmekkin'. Pity you ain't stoppin' twothri days — I'd lend you a rod and you could have a go at the roach in the brook. There's a tidy hole or two there. Now and then you'll git a jack too."

It was not quite dark when they went to bed. She stood for a few moments at the window of her room, watching the red rows of bean flowers, the white and purple of peas and potatoes, as they melted into shadow.

"There's a thrush still singing. That's late in the summer," she said.

She took off her shoes and stockings and walked about the room in her bare feet. The door between the rooms was open. She unbuttoned the neck of her dress and began to take it off and then he was standing at the door.

"Let me do it," he said.

She let him undress her in the darkness. He was trembling and clumsy in tenderness and once he said:

"I wish it wasn't dark now. I wish I could see you."

He touched her and she began trembling too. Outside in the darkened garden the thrush was no longer singing. As he came close to her she put out of her mind every thought of what might still happen; but in a moment of anguish he remembered it:

"What about tomorrow? — what's going to happen tomorrow?"

"Never mind about tomorrow."

"They're bound to be after us — "

"Don't think about it. That doesn't matter," she said. She spoke softly, drawing him to her. "You're with me. That's all that matters."

Some time later he lay wide-eyed, quivering, in an agony of sweat.

"They could hang me," he said. "Supposing they hang me?"

"They'll never do that," she said. In the darkness she

shrouded him with her naked body. It was the first time she had ever thought of hanging. Now it went through her mind like the leap of an ugly rat. "That's something they'll never do." With difficulty she kept from screaming out. "That's something they'll never do."

For some time she heard him weeping with shame and distress in the darkness. The sobbing of his voice was harsh and dry. With deadly fear it echoed through her mind long after he had stopped crying and had gone to sleep in her arms:

"They could. You know they could. They could hang him. You know they could."

X

THEY stayed at the house, with the Sherwoods, in the island of garden surrounded by osier beds, for three nights and three days. Twice she woke early in the morning and looked up at a strange ceiling and wondered where she was. She lay listening to the first sounds of the day, the first before Sherwood let out the hens or took the swill bucket from the outhouse or slipped the chained staple from the cowshed door. The first sound was the light croak of moor hens wandering landward through the osier beds from the direction of the brook.

On the third morning she woke to a new sound, to what she thought at first was the drowsy turning of leaves throughout the entire mass of osier and willow and ash outside. Then she sat up in bed and looked at the garden. Rain in a fine summer mesh was falling, clinging to everything in misted pinhead beads.

She lay for a long time listening to this sound. It had the effect, once or twice, of a crowd of people whispering outside, and then presently of enshrouding her thoughts with calmness. She turned and lay on her back, moving quietly so that she should not wake him. She stared at the

ceiling and let her mind, for perhaps the twentieth time
or more, go carefully over all that had happened on Sunday afternoon.

"Nobody saw it only me," she would think. "I was
really the only one who saw it. When the time comes I've
only got to say what I saw. I've only got to tell the truth
and say what I saw and not change a word of it. I know
what I saw and nobody else knows and I'll never change
a word of what I say."

That morning she began to think of something else. She
had put out of her mind, for two days, any thought of the
sea. Now, because of something Sherwood had said the
previous evening, she allowed it to come back.

"Ain't very often as we do go out anywheres, but I got
two dozen baskets for a man in St. Neots as is bin a-prom-
ising to fetch 'em this three months. Thought I might
take 'em over. I could do wi' the money. And if you folks
are still going that way we could give you a ride that far.
Missus'll be coming with me and we s'll shut the house for
the day."

It seemed almost a hint, she thought, that it was time
to go.

"Friday," Sherwood said. "Git a start about ten o'clock."

As she lay thinking of this she was aware once again of
the curious personal whispering effect of the rain outside:
a sound as if people were actually gathering under the
window and talking softly. It was so strong that after some
moments she got out of bed and went to the window and
looked out.

There was nothing there but the mesh of summer morning rain caught on the pale green branches of peas in big silver drops, weighing down the heads of potato flower and darkening the red of bean blossom on tall thick rows. But when she got back into bed again and lay quietly for a time she was aware of the old irresistible effect of whispering gradually coming back.

People standing there, people whispering, somebody watching, she thought.

She thought of Sherwood. Perhaps, she thought, it was all a trick. When we first came here he said they never went out; now they're suddenly going out. They don't want us here. They're going to shut the house up. They're suspicious. They don't trust us, any more.

She listened again to the rain whispering outside. Some of her calmness left her for a moment or two and she thought of waking Con. Then when she turned to look at him she saw his face in a sleep of extraordinary quietness. His hands were drawing at the edges of the pillow and holding them against his mouth.

Then she thought: "I'm a fool. Let him sleep while he can. There's nobody there. Why should there be?"

She lay listening for some time longer, slightly uneasy in the enclosed world of rain. Then she heard Sherwood dropping the staple-chain at the door of the cowhouse, then the sound of a swill bucket set down and the yell of pigs in sties.

Con woke a moment later and turned and looked at her.

"I had a dream you went into a bakehouse for a loaf and they caught you and you never came out again."

"Not me," she said.

He listened. "What's that?"

"Rain," she said.

"I thought it was somebody talking outside."

"How did you sleep?" she said.

"I lay thinking a long time."

"Hold me," she said. "I've been waiting for you to wake up and hold me."

"I was thinking what they'd do to you," he said. "Will they do something to you?"

"Why should they?"

"They will," he said. "They'll say you were there and you were in it."

"They won't do anything to me," she said. "And they won't do anything to you either. They'll never get you. That's why."

She was uneasy all morning. She was glad when the rain slackened, lifted and finally left off at noon. By early afternoon the paths across the garden were steaming in sunshine and by five o'clock the garden was dry under a clear hot sky.

"Take the rod and have a go at the roach for a couple of hours," Sherwood said. "They oughta take a mite o' paste or bread crust — after that rain. Might even try a few elderberries. There's a good big tree a couple o' hundred yards up the brook."

"If he's goin' a-fishing," Mrs. Sherwood said, "you can

come along o' me and git currants. Blame me if I won't soon look like currants. Same every year — I'm glad when July's over."

She gathered red currants with Mrs. Sherwood until seven o'clock. As she came across the yard to the house she saw Sherwood taking straw to the cowhouse and called to ask if Con were back. "Not yit," Sherwood said. "Still temptin' on 'em."

She went into the kitchen. She washed the stain of currants from her hands and slipped upstairs for a moment to comb her hair. When she came down again she called to Sherwood that she was going to look for Con.

"I fancy he went upstream," he said. "There's a bit of a bridge there. You'll see. With a biggish hole underneath an elder tree the other side."

There was no one by the elder tree. She walked a hundred yards beyond it and stopped by the gate of a second field. The brook came down through open marshland covered with nothing but big tussocks of sedge and occasional water holes of reed. She could see for half a mile or more.

She walked back, past the bridge and then downstream for half a mile. The osier beds ended and gave way to a spinney of ash and hazel. Then the spinney ended and gave way to open meadow. The banks of the brook became flatter, without trees. A wire fence fringed part of one side of it. Two hundred yards away the water was so shallow that cows could ford it without wetting their hocks.

She looked across empty meadows for a minute or two and then turned back. Halfway back to the bridge she began to run. She did not open her mouth to call but all the time her mind was on the verge of a scream. All her uneasiness of the morning broke into fright.

"Con, where are you? Where have you got to? What's happened? Con? what's happened? Where are you, where are you?"

At the bridge she saw where he had stood to fish. A slice of bread and a few bullets of paste still lay on the stone parapet. A few balls of part-ripe elderberries were spread beside it. A crowd of big sandy flies rose from rain-softened pads of cow dung. The only other sound was a moor hen walking daintily among tall water grasses somewhere upstream.

"Con!" She began calling aloud. "Con! Are you there, Con?" She climbed the gate on the far side of the bridge and called once or twice into the field there. "Con! Aren't you there? Con!"

Then she saw the rod, dismantled and packed in its canvas case and leaning against the lower buttress of the bridge. A dead roach, five or six inches long, lay on the stones beside it.

She started running upstream. The moor hen, frightened, broke from the grasses and floundered into dark flight under shadows of alder. Then it hit water again and dived.

"Are you there, Con?" she yelled. "Con, where are you?"

She called for another five minutes or so, running and walking and stumbling up and down the banks of the stream. Then she remembered the rod. She picked it up and some of her calmness came back and she thought:

"He must have gone back and no one saw him. Perhaps he didn't feel well. Perhaps he was sick and didn't want to tell me."

She went back to the house and upstairs to the bedrooms. "Can't you find him nowhere?" Sherwood called but she was too distracted to stop or reply.

Both bedrooms were empty. She sat for some minutes on her bed, trying to think. Her mind was like a machine clicking over with the same repeated thought: "Con, where have you gone to? You wouldn't go away from me, now, would you? Where have you gone to, Con, where have you gone to?"

Then she got up from the bed. As she did so something slipped off the counterpane and rolled on the floor. She picked up a sovereign and stood staring at it in her hand.

She ran downstairs. She tried to speak calmly. "He must have been back. Didn't you see him come back? Were you here all the time?"

"I was back o' the barn there for a time. Opening a sack o' pollard — "

"He must have come back. He must have come back and gone out for something and we didn't see him."

Mrs. Sherwood came from the kitchen, wiping red-stained hands on a sack-apron.

"He went for a walk, very like. He could have walked up to the church."

"Church? What church?"

She pointed across the road, into the rise of fields, with their groups of cedar and beech and lime, beyond.

"Up through the park. Stands all by itself in the middle on it. There's a kiss-gate just up the road there and a footpath and you follow that."

"Be home for his supper any road," Sherwood said. "You can count on that."

"I'll back he will," Mrs. Sherwood said. "They ain't fur off, men ain't, when it's feed time."

She walked up to the church. She went inside and sat down and stared at the marble effigies, the fat cherubim and seraphim of family tombs, and knew that it was no use. It did not matter; there was no point in looking there. She sat in a pew and held her head in her hands while sparrows chattered at her from the porch outside.

"You couldn't have gone off like that, all of a sudden, unless it was something awful. Where are you, Con? For God's sake, where have you got to?"

Most of the night she lay wide awake, thinking the same thing, asking herself:

"Where could I start looking? I don't even know where to start looking. And the sovereign." She thought over and over again of the sovereign. It was the sovereign, more than anything else, that seemed to her a fatal key. "You'd never have left the sovereign for me if you were coming back."

Once she got out of bed and began to put on her stockings. She had an idea of dressing herself and going out
and walking up and down the road, but she had hardly
found the stockings in the darkness before she heard, once
again, the whisper of summer rain beginning to fall outside.

She got back into bed and lay listening to it: the same
curious half-real sound of gathering voices, of people
closing in, shuffling and whispering and enmeshing
her.

"What made you go without me?" she thought. "Why
did you?" She was remotely bitter, in anguish, with the
memory of Arch Wilson. "You wouldn't do that, would
you? Not like that. Like he did. After what we did together? Oh! Con, come back! Please come back."

Towards morning she dropped into a half-doze. When
she woke, in a dazed way, about eight o'clock, Mrs. Sherwood was in the room.

"Oh! you are awake. I never heard nothing on you."
She peered down obliquely through the window. "There's
a man downstairs."

"Man?"

"He wants to see you he says."

"Man? What man?"

"I don't know. He come in a horse and trap," she
said.

Bella went to the window and looked out. Rain was
falling quietly on an empty garden. Potato flowers were
drooping in white and purple curls. "He left the trap

outside," Mrs. Sherwood said. "I count he's gone back to that."

"I'll be down," she said.

Some minutes later, walking out of the garden, down the cart track, in the rain, she had a wild impression that Con had come back. A man with his back to her was standing at the gate, by a horse and trap, giving a handful of hay to the horse. It was only when he turned that she saw how mistaken she had been.

"Jedd," she said. "Jedd."

He came running towards her at the sound of her voice; he met her and held her by the hands.

"Jedd, what brings you here? What is it? How did you know?"

"He come home," Jedd said. "Just afore five o'clock this morning. He come to give himself up."

The horse was a dark chestnut, with a dab of cream on the side of one ear. As they drove home she stared continually at this touch of lightness on the rain-wet brown of the horse. After a mile or two the rain came on a little heavier and faster and Jedd put up the big cart umbrella against it and she said:

"That's heavy for you. I'll help you hold it."

She put her hands with his on the thick bamboo handle of the umbrella. His hands were rough and wet with rain. The veins on the backs of them stood raised up and stiff and quivering.

"I never slept for a week," he said. "I couldn't sleep for thinking about you."

She sat still, calmer than she had been at any moment since the previous day and stared at the dab of cream on the ear of the horse as it flicked through the rain.

"Did he do it?" Jedd asked.

In her calmness she was sitting upright, so much in the way she often walked, head up and thrown a little backward, that she seemed to have on her face almost a look of defiance.

"I'll tell all about it," she said, "when the time comes."

His hands began quaking and convulsing on the bamboo handle of the umbrella.

"I got something to tell you," he said. "I think they want you too."

There was no alteration in her look of upright calm. She looked through the rain to the flicking ear of the horse. She stared beyond it to the summer country drowned in summer rain.

"I can only tell what happened. I can only tell the truth," she said. "Don't be frightened and don't ask me anything. I can't tell you any more."

X I

SHE was walking down into the valley, alone again, carrying the small dress case in which were all her things. It was late October. The thin stunted oaks in the small copses were smoldering wet and brown after night-rain. The long bare sky line was bright blue and sometimes the smoke of trains steaming across a viaduct below her drooped into the full river like falling clouds.

"I'd rather go by myself. I'd rather go alone. I've got plenty of time for the train and it would be better if you didn't come with me."

She had given herself more than half an hour to walk to the station. As she changed the dress basket from hand to hand she did not hurry. And once as she stopped to tie her shoelace she remembered how also, in almost the same place, she had stopped to tie her hair. Below her, all the time, in the center of the bare valley, by the river, she could see the station. It was not the station where Con had once waited for her by the footbridge, putting out the light. Trains from there went southward. This was the old station: the station for the east, the fenlands and the sea.

"Do you recall a particular occasion, Mr. Faulkner, when you went to Nenweald and paid a visit to the Wharf public house there?"

"Yes, sir."

"That was in the summer of last year, was it not?"

"Yes, sir. About the third Saturday in June."

"The precise date is really immaterial. What I am really concerned to establish is what happened to you yourself on that occasion. Am I right in saying that you were on that occasion subjected to a most unpleasant and unprovoked attack?"

"That's right, sir."

"Mr. Faulkner, I want you to take a good look round the court. Take your time. Look carefully and then tell the court if you recognize here any person whom you remember as being the author of that attack."

"Him — there."

"You mean the accused — Wainwright? The prisoner?"

"Yessir."

"Now take another look. Do you recognize any other person who was present during that attack?"

"Yessir. Her. The witness Ford."

"One more thing, Mr. Faulkner. Although that attack is now some fifteen or sixteen months ago is your recollection of it sufficiently clear to assist the court in another matter? Would you, in fact, remember the name by which the accused called you in that alarming attack on your person?"

"Yessir."

"Then will you be so good as to tell the court what it was?"

"Wilson, sir. Arch Wilson."

"Thank you, Mr. Faulkner."

Over in the fields to her left she could see a yellow-white ring of stones: all that remained of the mill on the backwater. She remembered how she and Con had ridden the boat there, under the tunnel on the far side of the mill-race, that Sunday afternoon. At the same moment she remembered the butterflies, the clouds of brown and blue sparking and smoking from thistle flower, the crowd of dragonflies crackling from reeds, the bees with yellow heads that did not sting. She remembered how, that day, Con had asked her to marry him and how happy she had been.

"You are, I believe, the billiard marker at The Angel Hotel at Bedford?"

"Yes."

"And do you recall, on the first Saturday of July last, acting as marker to the late unfortunate Mr. Wilson?"

"I do."

"Anything remarkable about the game?"

"Mr. Wilson left the game for five minutes to talk to a young lady out in the passage. When he come back he was all over himself and kept saying 'Bella. My God, young Bella. Who would have thought it?' and all like that."

"Never mind about all like that. Be good enough to recall, if you can, anything further Mr. Wilson said of

Miss Ford and repeat it for the benefit of the court as precisely as you can."

"I heard him say 'She's over at Nenweald. I'm going over there tomorrow.' "

"You are quite sure it was tomorrow — that is, the Sunday?"

"Positive, your honor."

"I am not your honor. But thank you all the same. That will do."

She watched a goods train puffing up the valley. Its smoke, curving downward, grayish-white, making a series of curls, reminded her suddenly of all the wigs, too many for her to count, that for three days had moved backwards and forwards before her, in and out of the court.

"Your brother, on that occasion, made an astonishing and violent attack on you in the harvest field?"

"It was in fun."

"In what? What did you say? In fun? Do you sincerely ask the court to believe that an attack with a naked scythe is something indulged in for fun?"

"We was always at it. The pair of us. I never took no notice on it. It was Mum who took the notice. She run us round the field and threatened to thresh our arses."

"That will do, Mr. Wainwright. Moderate your language. Remember you are in court."

"Sorry, sir. I'm a soldier."

She remembered and thought with great affection of Jedd. Jedd at first in terror that she, too, would be charged; Jedd in distress at the pain of others, talking

over and over again of "Accessory. That's what they call
it. Accessory before the fact. It means you and Con laid
your heads together." And then Jedd knowing she was
not to be charged, hardening and calming himself, the
soldier disciplined, the soldier ready to face the moment
of final crisis.

"Mrs. Wainwright, you have heard described the incident of your eldest son attacking his brother with a scythe
in the harvest field. You were present on that occasion,
I believe?"

"Yes, sir."

"Would you describe that as a vicious and unprovoked
attack?"

"It was just like him."

"You mean it was like your eldest son to display un-
governable temper?"

"When he gets set on anything you can't turn him."

"Set on anything, Mrs. Wainwright?"

"Yes, sir. When he sets his heart on anything it ain't a
mite o' use you goin' against him. I were fool enough to
try once or twice and I know. I recollect the time he used
to collect butterflies — "

"Thank you, Mrs. Wainwright. I do not think the court
wants to hear about butterflies."

At the bottom of the hill, where the road flattened out
to cross the valley, the leaves of a line of pollard willows
on the side of a walled meadow were falling like shoals
of pale yellow fish on to the road, the field and a stretch
of backwater beyond. Halfway along the backwater a

man with a long black jacket and deep flopping poacher's pockets was casting a line. She set her dress case on the stone parapet of the wall and watched the scarlet float fly out across the water. She saw the float bob upright, showing only the cap of the quill.

"You knew the late Mr. Wilson, I believe I am right in saying, before you came to live at Nenweald?"

"I did know him. Yes."

"Am I right in saying that you were then on terms of some intimacy with him?"

"Yes."

"That he was, in fact, your lover?"

"Yes."

"More than that — that he was, in fact, the father of your child?"

"Yes."

"Was Mr. Wilson aware of that fact?"

"He was not the sort of man to worry about a little thing like that."

"I am not concerned, Miss Ford, with whether he was worried about your unfortunate condition. Did he know?"

"He did not."

"Did the accused, Con Wainwright, know?"

"He did."

"Now, Miss Ford. Prior to the fatal incident on the river on Sunday afternoon can you tell us when was the last time you saw Mr. Wilson?"

"The Saturday. The previous day."

"And before that?"

"About two years before."

"About two years before. So it comes, doesn't it, to this? Less than twenty-four hours after you meet Mr. Wilson for the first time for two years he is lying dead at your feet after a violent quarrel with the accused? Doesn't that strike you as an extraordinarily swift and remarkable co-incidence?"

"No."

"I suggest to you that it is. I suggest to you that you heard your former lover say that he was coming to Nen-weald and that you then told the accused so that he should be ready to — shall we say? — give him a lesson? I put it to you, in fact, that the accused knew of his coming and was waiting?"

"He did not know."

"Can you tell us why did he not know?"

"Because I didn't tell him."

"And can you tell us why didn't you tell him?"

"I didn't wish him to know. I was afraid for what might happen."

"And what were you afraid might happen? Exactly, I suggest, what did happen — that this unfortunate gentle-man, quietly angling on a Sunday afternoon, should sud-denly without warning be struck to his death by a person of jealous and violent disposition? A man, as we have heard, who could not be turned or thwarted when his mind was set to an end?"

"There was no need for him to know," she said. "What was gone was gone. It was in the past. It was all forgiven and forgotten. We were very happy."

She watched the float delicately drawn in, like a little stiff red-and-white fish, making a quick light furrow on the rain-darkened water. She watched for a moment or two longer as the man with the poacher's pockets pinched on to the hook another grain of bait. She saw him make a new cast with a high arc of his arm. Then as the float popped again she picked up her dress basket and walked on. She had another quarter of a mile to go.

"And Wilson, you say, was the first to strike a blow?"

"Yes."

"You say with the chair? In fact with this chair?"

"Yes."

"Can you say how many blows? One blow or several?"

"One, at first."

"You seem very sure of that. Can you tell us why?"

"Because he pinched his fingers. Like you did just now."

"Silence!" the ushers called.

"We now come to a further point. If this tragic affair was the outcome of a quarrel — a quarrel in which there was something coincidental if not accidental — why did you not seek some sort of aid for this unfortunate man? Why, if there was nothing to fear and nothing to answer, did you run away?"

"You would not understand that," she said.

A rise of cloud from the west had begun to give the sky

great brilliance, pure strong blue after the wash of rain. As she came to the bridge she saw the seven arches of it turn shadowy and light with the run of a cloud. The water reflected the blue and white of sky with freshness and clearness, the stone arrows of the bridge buttresses making white feathers of foam where the current pressed against them.

"You must then give most careful attention to the testimony of Bella Ford. You may think, and I believe you would be right to think, that hers is the most important testimony of all that has been given in this case. You may think too that she was not only an important witness but also, in several ways, a remarkable one. It may have struck you that she gave her evidence in a way that was exceptionally straightforward, lucid and unshaken. You may think that she showed herself to be a person of strong mind and strong devotion who would let nothing interfere with her intention of telling the facts as she saw them. You may think that she was very honest on occasions when it is very painful for a woman to be honest, and if it is in your minds that at least some part of her attitude is inspired by her love of the accused that is a point on which I would not wish to influence you to think otherwise."

A train, bellying white-gray smoke, coming up the valley on the flat open line that ran beside dykes of feathering reed, gave a whistle that startled her. She looked ahead of her to see the gates of the level crossing closing, white-barred with central circles of red, across the road.

"In short, there were times when she seemed to be by far the calmest person here. You may have thought, in fact, that she was at her calmest when answering the most critical question of all — the question put to her by Mr. Bellingham-Lloyd as to whether or not she had told the accused that she had met Wilson on the eve of that fateful Sunday. It may have been very tempting for her to lie on that point: to say 'No' because, in her case, to say 'Yes' would be by far the more damning answer. Yet you may not have failed to notice that her reason for not telling the accused about it caused her ultimately to give what seemed to be a still more damning answer — namely 'I didn't tell him. I was afraid for what might happen.' "

The train in the station blew into the brilliant morning blue of the sky a column of smoke as straight as a white poplar.

"Then there is the testimony of Mr. Harry Turner, the landlord of the Wharf public house, and it is a testimony that has great importance in determining the attitude, movements and condition of Wilson on that Sunday. In the landlord's own words 'Wilson had had enough by three o'clock and was getting over his collar.' There is a great deal of drunkenness on this Sunday of the Big Feast and normally it does not come to much more than sore heads and fisticuffs. Wilson was in the company of a man named Flawn and according to the evidence of Mr. Harry Turner the two men were aggressive and argumentative and in fighting mood. Fortunately or unfortunately Wilson and Flawn decided, in Flawn's own words, 'to go and have a poke at the jack,' in other words to go fishing for pike up the river. That is the last thing the witness Flawn remembers, for he fell down in a drunken coma before he left the gentlemen's convenience in the yard."

The train, she thought, seemed to be standing a long time in the station. Its white column of steam, blown straight up into the blue October air, was still rising as she reached the level crossing gates and stood there waiting for the train to go. It would not be more than another five minutes, she thought, before her own train arrived.

"There is, as I have told you, the question of motive and there is also, which you must weigh most carefully, the question of provocation. Was there motive? Was there premeditation? Was there provocation? These are all things for you and not for me. I can only direct you in these matters. It is for you, and you alone, to decide if this is a case of wilful murder. But if there is any reasonable doubt in your minds — "

Across the line, through the bars of the level crossing gates, she saw a figure lifting a hand. It seemed to be waving at her. Before it could wave a second time the train drew forward on the tracks, between the gates, and shut it away.

Then the train was pulling along the line and the gates were swinging back. A cloud of steam and smoke hung over the station, was caught in a stir of wind and lifted. The figure came across the line, taking off its hat.

"Matty."

[241]

"I've got your ticket," he said.

He took the dress basket from her hands.

"I think she's signaled."

They walked up the ramp of the far platform and stood there waiting for the train. For some moments she did not know what to say. A down-line signal clattered on several hundred yards away, frightening a dozen rooks from the tops of the telegraph wires.

"You shouldn't have got my ticket," she said.

"It wasn't me. He told me I had to."

"You'd better give it to me," she said. "The gates are closing again."

"I'm coming a little way with you," he said. "Just three or four stations. He said I had to."

When the train came in he opened a carriage door and she got in. He followed and put her dress basket on the seat. Then he sat opposite her and said:

"Did you mind me coming?"

"You know I wouldn't mind."

"I'm glad," he said.

"I'm glad too," she said. "I can't tell you how glad I feel."

As the train moved away between rain-filled dykes of reed, crossing the river occasionally and then leaving it again, crowds of rooks and jackdaws and sometimes a flock of starlings, gathering for winter, rose from wet meadows and planed away in the fresh clear sky.

"Do you still want to go?" he said. "You don't have to go. You could stay with us."

"It'll be better. I shall be better with my sister. Away from things."

"Ten years is a long time."

"It won't seem so long. Not so long as some times I've known."

"Will you come back and see us sometimes?"

"Sometimes I suppose I will. When I —"

"Christmas or Easter — or the Feast," he said.

"Not the Feast," she said.

During most of this time she sat staring from the window. It was only after the train had stopped at the third station down the line that she noticed he had a parcel in his hands.

"This is for you," he said.

"For me? Who from?"

"From Con," he said. "Shoes."

She took the parcel from him and laid it on the seat.

"Be sure to put it with your dress basket," he said, "then you won't forget it. I wanted to make them myself," he went on, "but there wasn't time."

"The river's full after the rain," she said. "It's wide and lovely here."

"I shall have to get out at the next station," he said. "I wish you'd change your mind and come back."

"No," she said. "Not now."

"I can't help thinking you'll be lonely by yourself. Up there."

"I shan't be lonely," she said. "My sister will be good to me. She's a good soul. I was lonely when I came here, but I'm not now. I shan't be. I've got a lot to do. I shall have a lot to think about."

The train and the river converged, running side by side. She could see on the surface of the river a few bright pads of water lilies, untouched by frost, still green after summer. A moor hen scuttled and dived past them at the sound of the train. And suddenly she remembered the sound of moor hens making their light creaking talk in the osier beds, at the Sherwoods', when she first woke in the mornings.

Then the train slowed down.

"There's just something I wanted to say," he said. "If I hadn't let Con talk round me that night at the station things might have — "

"No, they wouldn't," she said. "It wasn't anything to do with you. It was only me. If I hadn't come down here — that's what you ought to say. If I hadn't come down here, saying I'd kill Arch Wilson."

"Kill him?"

"I didn't know what I was saying, but I said I would kill him," she said. "And I meant it then."

"Oh! my God. Oh! Bella," he said.

Just before the train stopped he got up. He suddenly stooped and kissed her. In a moment of unconscious response, without thinking, she put up her hands and held them flatly against his. She felt once again the small pulsing beats of her blood throbbing against the small fingers and then she drew away her face and said:

"Whenever I think of you I shall think of your small hands."

"Think often," he said.

"Often and often," she said. "Of course I shall. I've got a lot to think of."

From the carriage windows she leaned out and kissed him again. For the second time she touched his hands. Tears waiting to fall from the lids of his eyes gave his face a remarkable brightness.

"Don't forget the shoes," he said and began to wave his hand.

"I shan't forget."

She waved too; the wind of the moving train blew her dark hair crosswise into her face, into her eyes, and she held her hair with one hand while waving with the other.

As the train went on she sat still, in the corner of the carriage, watching the water-freshened meadows, the river closing in towards the railway track, the rooks and jack-daws rising from the telegraph wires and circling blackly over the fields.

After a time she closed her eyes. She sat with her hands clasped together in front of her. The pulse of blood that had been stimulated a few minutes before by Matty's hands seemed to grow stronger as she sat there.

Then presently she knew that it was not merely in her hands. It had begun to enlarge and repeat itself inside her body. It stirred with the movement of a muscle stiffening and then relaxing. It fluttered several times and then quietened again. Finally it turned more sharply and she knew there was no mistaking it.

She opened her eyes and looked at the river. Beyond it, on roads and in copses, there were trees, mostly elms, that were still dark green with the leaves of summer. Across all the meadows, between dykes and hedgerows, the grass was as thick and green as it had been after the silt of floods had fed it in spring.

"Lie still now," she said. "Lie still. I know you're there."

She smiled and shut her eyes. The carriage was warm with October sunshine. On her face was a look of great contentment and her thoughts were of the sea.

VINTAGE INTERNATIONAL

POSSESSION
by A. S. Byatt

An intellectual mystery and a triumphant love story of a pair of young scholars researching the lives of two Victorian poets.

"Gorgeously written . . . a tour de force." —*The New York Times Book Review*

Winner of the Booker Prize
Fiction/Literature/0-679-73590-9

THE STRANGER
by Albert Camus

Through the story of an ordinary man who unwittingly gets drawn into a senseless murder, Camus explores what he termed "the nakedness of man faced with the absurd."

Fiction/Literature/0-679-72020-0

INVISIBLE MAN
by Ralph Ellison

This searing record of a black man's journey through contemporary America reveals, in Ralph Ellison's words, "the sheer rhetorical challenge involved in communicating across our barriers of race and religion, class, color and region."

"The greatest American novel in the second half of the twentieth century...the classic representation of American black experience." —R.W. B. Lewis

Fiction/Literature/0-679-72313-7

THE REMAINS OF THE DAY
by Kazuo Ishiguro

A profoundly compelling portrait of the perfect English butler and of his fading, insular world in postwar England.

"One of the best books of the year." —*The New York Times Book Review*

Fiction/Literature/0-679-73172-5

ALL THE PRETTY HORSES
by Cormac McCarthy

At sixteen, John Grady Cole finds himself at the end of a long line of Texas ranchers, cut off from the only life he has ever imagined for himself. With two companions, he sets off for Mexico on a sometimes idyllic, sometimes comic journey, to a place where dreams are paid for in blood.

"A book of remarkable beauty and strength, the work of a master in perfect command of his medium." —*Washington Post Book World*

Winner of the National Book Award for Fiction
Fiction/Literature/0-679-74439-8

BUDDENBROOKS
THE DECLINE OF A FAMILY
by Thomas Mann
Translated by John E. Woods

This masterpiece is an utterly absorbing chronicle of four generations of a German mercantile family. As Thomas Mann charts the Buddenbrooks' decline, he creates a world of exuberant vitality and almost Rabelaisian earthiness.

"Wonderfully fresh and elegant . . . bound to become the definitive English version."
—*Los Angeles Times*

Fiction/Literature/0-679-75260-9

LOLITA
by Vladimir Nabokov

The famous and controversial novel that tells the story of the aging Humbert Humbert's obsessive, devouring, and doomed passion for the nymphet Dolores Haze.

"The only convincing love story of our century."
—*Vanity Fair*

Fiction/Literature/0-679-72316-1

THE ENGLISH PATIENT
by Michael Ondaatje

During the final moments of World War II, four damaged people come together in a deserted Italian villa. As their stories unfold, a complex tapestry of image and emotion, recollection and observation is woven.

"It seduces and beguiles us with its many-layered mysteries, its brilliantly taut and lyrical prose, its tender regard for its characters."
—*Newsday*

Winner of the Booker Prize
Fiction/Literature/0-679-74520-3

OPERATION SHYLOCK
by Philip Roth

In this tour de force of fact and fiction, Philip Roth meets a man who may or may not be Philip Roth. Because *someone* with that name has been touring the State of Israel, promoting a bizarre exodus in reverse, and it is up to Roth to stop him—even if that means impersonating his impersonator.

"A diabolically clever, engaging work . . .the result is a kind of dizzying exhilaration."
—*Boston Globe*

Fiction/Literature/0-679-75029-0

VINTAGE INTERNATIONAL

AVAILABLE AT YOUR LOCAL BOOKSTORE, OR CALL TOLL-FREE TO ORDER: 1-800-793-2665 (CREDIT CARDS ONLY).